Jessica kissed Aaron, deeply and hungrily.

Her skin was so sensitive that every movement caused tremors of excitement to flow through her. She could feel that his body was rock hard against her.

The elevator dinged and the doors slid open, but as she began to pull away to exit, the arm wrapped around her waist tightened and held her against him, her feet hovering above the floor, his lips still on her. He had lifted her enough so he could kiss along her jawline and her neck, and stepped off the elevator with her in his arms, making her feel as though tiny explosions were going off in her brain.

"What room?" he growled into her neck, letting loose waves of electricity in the spots warmed by his breath.

A tingle went down her spine as she heard the complete abandon in his voice.

He wasn't in control of himself, and she had the feeling it wasn't something that happened to him very often.

And, oh, she liked it...

Dear Reader,

This book was a work of pure enjoyment for me. I never thought I'd actually write a book, but after living in Vegas for so many years, the idea of writing about this unique city and the people who travel here became an itch I finally decided to scratch. As a local, the tourism of Las Vegas is a wonderful opportunity for people watching and story invention, and I constantly find myself wondering about the backgrounds and futures of the people who breeze in and out for a few days of fun.

Writing about the rodeo in particular seemed like the perfect topic, with the annual influx of attractive cowboys. On our nightly walks during that unique week, my husband and I found ourselves passing hundreds of cowboys, and I couldn't help but create stories about what they would do while visiting Sin City, and who they might meet along the way. The seed of an idea was born. It was an exciting moment, the first day I sat down with my laptop and began *Her Sexy Vegas Cowboy*.

I hope you enjoy reading about Aaron and Jessica. I loved writing about them, and about this wonderful city that so few have the opportunity to truly explore.

Cheers,

Ali Olson

Ali Olson

Her Sexy Vegas Cowboy

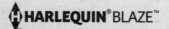

Recycling programs
for this product may
not exist in your area.

ISBN-13: 978-0-373-79881-0

Her Sexy Vegas Cowboy

Printed in U.S.A.

™ www.Harlequin.com

Ali Olson is a longtime resident of Las Vegas, Nevada, where she has been teaching English at the high school and college level for the past seven years. Ali has found a passion for writing sexy romance novels, both contemporary and historical, and is enthusiastic about her newly discovered career. She loves reading, writing and traveling with her husband and constant companion, Joe. She appreciates hearing from readers. Write to her at authoraliolson.com.

To get the inside scoop on Harlequin Blaze and its talented writers, be sure to check out BlazeAuthors.com.

All backlist available in ebook format.

Visit the Author Profile page at Harlequin.com for more titles.

For Mary, who has been my biggest fan as long as I can remember and supported me in every endeavor. Thank you for always believing so strongly in my abilities.

And Joe, thank you for always being so sure I was a brilliant writer and would be successful. Life with you is the best adventure.

JESSICA GAINEY LEANED against the window of the airplane, watching the ground as they slowly descended into Las Vegas. She'd been to the city before, but had never flown over it at night, when Vegas was a bright spot of lights and civilization surrounded on all sides by a sea of blackness. On every side, the desert hemmed in the oasis of streetlights and hotels.

Along the famous Strip, Las Vegas Boulevard, she recognized some of the big casinos and icons like the Stratosphere and Luxor pyramid with its bright light shooting up into space and wondered at the changes in the constantly shifting city. There was a huge Ferris wheel lit up in bright colors. Since when did Vegas have a Ferris wheel?

As she continued to soak up the sight of the bright city, the plane touched down at McCarran Airport, which seemed to be right in the middle of it all. She settled back into her seat for the slow taxi to the terminal, closing her eyes and enjoying the last few moments before the insanity would begin.

The flight had been relatively quiet, since she'd purchased a coach ticket despite Cindy's willingness to pay the extra costs so she could sit in first class with the rest of the party. It had actually been a perfect time for her to get a little work done before the long weekend, which she was fairly sure would include out-of-control partying by the large group of former sorority sisters currently sitting together in the front of the plane. She was already exhausted at the idea and nothing had happened yet.

She pushed her worries away, turned on her phone's Wi-Fi, and quickly scanned her emails and texts. She knew there would be no messages from Russ, but she still hadn't broken the habit of looking for them. When they were together, he'd always write little love notes to her while she was flying, making her phone ping with joy when she turned it on after landing. It had been such a sweet gesture and she hadn't flown enough since then to adjust to its absence.

Those messages had caused the ending of their relationship, but she definitely didn't want to think about that. She'd spent enough time in the past few months reliving the moment when she opened his phone to see the exact wording of a recent text from Russ that she'd accidentally deleted, only to find messages to other women alongside hers.

Jessica breathed in deeply and tried to let go of those negative thoughts, but the memories of that day were still impossible to banish completely. The best she could do was ignore them and focus on more important things. The texts on her phone were all from her family now.

Her mom saying, "Your dad will be fine. Have fun!"

Her sister telling her, "Relax. I know you freak out. Don't freak out."

And finally one from her father. "Love you, Jess. Do something crazy for a change!"

As if that would happen.

She'd told herself to relax, make this a fun weekend, hundreds of times throughout the flight, but nothing would ever completely stop her anxiety. She always felt as though disaster would occur the minute she left the state.

This weekend was for Cindy, not her, and Cindy had done enough for her that she wasn't about to ruin this trip with all her negative thoughts. If Cindy hadn't taken her in and given her a place to stay, who knew where she would have lived the past three months? So here she was, in Las Vegas for her best friend's party, and she would try to enjoy it even if it killed her.

When the seat belt light turned off, Jessica grabbed her purse from beneath the seat, shoved herself into the crush of passengers waiting to get off and pulled down her carry-on bag. She could pretend to be a party girl for a few days and take a break from real life. She'd try, at least.

In the terminal, it was easy to find Cindy, since she was the only one surrounded by a small crowd of women in their midtwenties, all of whom were giggling like teenagers as they plastered Cindy with bachelorette paraphernalia, including a plastic tiara and a sash, all pink and covered in rhinestones.

Cindy smiled and struck a pose, the rhinestones catching the light. "How do I look?"

Jessica gave her a quick appraisal. "It's bachelorette-party chic, all right. You look like a woman who's going to be given a lot of free drinks."

Cindy looked ecstatic. "Perfect! Then let's get going!"

One woman in the party, a raven-haired beauty whose name Jessica couldn't for the life of her remember, piped up. "Before we hit baggage claim, I want to stop at the bathroom and fix my makeup. I'm sure I look awful."

As the other women assured their friend that she was beautiful and started to search out a bathroom, Jessica looked over the group . They all looked ready for a night on the town in their high heels and makeup and styled hair, still perfectly coiffed even after the long flight. She tugged at her long unruly hair, hoping it looked more or less acceptable. She thought of herself as decently pretty, but compared to them, she probably *did* look awful.

Jessica had known she would be an outsider as the only nonsorority sister there. She had hoped college was far enough in the past to make the difference less noticeable, but it was just as pronounced as it had ever been back then. She joined them, trying to make herself feel a part of this group.

The women trooped into the bathroom, but Cindy walked up to Jessica and wrapped an arm around her friend. "Thanks again for coming this weekend."

"It'll be fun."

Cindy snorted. "You're away from your family with a bunch of my sorority sisters in Las Vegas, where we'll be going to bars and clubs way past your bedtime. I think I know you well enough to say that this isn't your idea of fun. But thanks for coming anyway."

Jessica couldn't help smiling at that. Cindy knew her too well. "You make me sound like a grandma."

"Not a grandma, just a slightly agoraphobic, introverted worrywart."

"Because that's so much better?"

"Try to enjoy this weekend a little bit is all I'm saying."

Jessica looked at her friend, properly decorated for her weekend of debauchery, giving her begging eyes. Jessica did not want to be the reason Cindy wasn't happy on her big weekend. "I'll have fun, I promise. We're celebrating your wedding, after all. You only have two weeks left of the single life, so we better make the most of it."

"Thirteen days, seventeen hours and ten minutes, but who's counting?" Cindy said, grinning.

Jessica was happy her friend had found the love of her life. She really was. But that didn't stop her from feeling a twinge of jealousy. She wasn't anywhere close to that, and nothing made that stand out starker than her best friend's bliss.

The group reassembled and turned toward baggage claim, making their way through the maze of the airport. Jessica followed along, wheeling her small bag behind her, falling to the back of the crowd as they all chatted. For a few minutes, she tried to remember the names Cindy had thrown at her before they left.

"We have got the best weekend planned for you, Cindy. Just you wait!" gushed a gorgeous brunette. Alexis, probably. Jessica was pretty sure Cindy had mentioned an Alexis.

"It's going to be way better than that time we went to DC. There's no rain in Vegas," another woman said, and the rest agreed.

Jessica didn't know that woman's name, either, but she thought Cindy had told her something about her being in pageants. Miss New York and crazy titles like that. She was beautiful enough for it to be believable. In fact, they were all beautiful. What was the deal with that?

While she let her mind wander, the topic had drifted to their adventures in DC. Jessica didn't have any idea when that had happened. It must've been at some point during college, when she and Cindy drifted apart for a while. Cindy had done the sorority thing and the friends thing. Jessica had done the study and work-menial-jobs thing.

It struck Jessica that she and Cindy had led very different lives for quite a long time, and their circles of friends were incredibly different. Cindy was surrounded by laughing beautiful women who loved her. Jessica had Cindy, a few acquaintances and her family. Who on earth would be invited to her bachelorette party?

Not that she was anywhere close to getting married, and even if she was, she doubted she'd even have a party. Not her style. Still, the answer to that question was rather depressing. She tried to focus on anything else as she tagged along with the group.

People-watching was always something she enjoyed, inventing stories for the various individuals as they passed in and out of her life. It was a good way to quiet unpleasant thoughts. Jessica concentrated her attention on the groups of people arriving from around the country to spend a few days in this crazy city, wondering what their stories were.

As they walked through the airport, Jessica began to notice something odd. Not the people sitting at slot machines—though those were unusual for any other airport, they only seemed fitting here. No, this was something she'd never expected to see in Sin City: there were cowboys. Like, *a lot* of them.

Had Vegas turned in its strip clubs and casinos for ranches and horses or something?

She sped up slightly so she could catch up to the brunette—the others called her Anna, not Alexis. "Do you know why it looks like we're on the film set of a spaghetti Western?"

"Oh yeah, there's supposed to be a rodeo in town. I saw it on the hotel websites. Apparently it's this big deal, like the World Series of Rodeos or something," Anna responded.

Jessica allowed herself to drift to the back of the group again. A rodeo in Vegas. What a strange concept.

As she walked, she continued to stare at the mob of cowboys. She just couldn't help herself—it was such an odd sight. Then her eyes landed on a muscled, sun-browned man with blond hair falling into his incredibly blue eyes. He was putting on his own cowboy hat as he left the gate of his just-arrived airplane only a few feet away from her. Jessica couldn't help staring at him, the epitome of strength and ruggedness.

He really did seem as if he should be in a Western film. He was more than just attractive; he was swoon-worthy, knight-in-shining-armor *hot*.

Then he looked right at her and their eyes locked. She'd been caught red-handed, practically drooling over him. She froze like a deer in headlights.

The glance lasted only a couple of seconds, but Jessica would have sworn it was far longer. The thrill of heat that rushed through her as the stranger met her eyes made her heart miss a beat—and the heel of her shoe slip sideways.

Her attention rudely brought back to reality, she wobbled uncertainly for a moment, but managed to regain her balance instead of falling over completely. Her slightly twisted ankle sent a small jab of pain up her leg as she stepped down, angry at her inattention. She stepped on it more gingerly, glad her loose hair had fallen in front of her face and hidden the blush that came from realizing she'd been caught gawking at this stranger, and then nearly fallen over to top it all off.

"Are you okay?"

She looked up, praying it wasn't the handsome cowboy who had asked.

Of course, it was the handsome cowboy. And now he was even closer, practically touching her, with a smirk of amusement on his face. This couldn't get any worse. Adrenaline pumped through her, making her skin prickle—or maybe that was just her reaction to the man standing in front of her, his eyes burning into hers.

Then his smile widened, as if she had made some sort of joke. Or been the butt of a joke. It was probably the latter, since nothing seemed amusing about this situation.

He raised his eyebrows. "So, you're okay?"

He'd been waiting for her to answer. And instead she had stared at him like an idiot. If the power to become invisible could be summoned through wishes, she would have disappeared.

She was still very much visible, though. Jessica looked down at her feet, hoping he thought she was examining her ankle, but mostly to keep herself from losing herself in his eyes again. "I'm fine," she squeaked, her voice an entire octave above normal.

Well, it was better than absolute silence, at any rate.

The rumble of his laughter rolled through her. "How about I give you a ride to your hotel? Save you the taxi fare."

Part of Jessica—the pit of her stomach and her tingling fingers—wanted to take the sexy cowboy's offer, but most of her only wanted to get away as quickly as she could. She looked up and realized that Cindy and the rest of the women were far ahead. Apparently none of them had nearly fallen all over themselves over any attractive cowboys. "I'm with a group. In fact, I should go catch up to them."

Before she could move away, though, he pulled a pen and a thick book out of the pocket of his bag, took a torn piece of paper out of it that he was clearly using for a bookmark and started writing on it. "Well, if you find yourself with some free time this weekend, call me. We can have dinner."

She said the only coherent thing her brain could muster. "That was your bookmark."

He handed it to her, smiling. "Yep. Lost my place. Worth it if you call."

Jessica was having difficulty breathing. If she didn't get away from this man immediately, she might jump on him right there and make a scene for the entire airport. She shoved the paper into her pants pocket, mostly to keep herself from opening it to check that there was, in fact, a phone number written on it.

Without looking at him again, she turned to search for her glittery mob of women, purposely keeping her eyes averted. His eyes were still on her, though—she could feel them boring into her. Her group, far ahead, was still walking toward the exit. They hadn't seemed to notice her disappearance. A quickly mumbled "Thanks" was all she could manage, along with one last peek into his eyes, which were still focused on her.

Adjusting her grip on her suitcase handle, she rushed to catch up to Cindy and her friends, limping slightly. She did not turn to look at the stranger again, though a part of her wanted to get just one more glance before he disappeared from her life, if only to make sure he was as handsome as she thought. A picture of him would be nice. Maybe a kiss, too.

Jessica was shocked at the thoughts that were running through her head. It had been some time since she was with a man—she hadn't dated at all since Russ—

and this was the first time she felt anything close to desire in three months. And it had knocked her flat. She could picture the cowboy's eyes looking back at her, his strong arms wrapping around her waist...

She shook her head slightly, trying to get back under control. She would never see him again, so there was no point fantasizing about him. There was absolutely no way she would be meeting a stranger for dinner, even if he was incredibly handsome and had a voice that sent shivers snaking down her spine.

If her crazy attraction toward this stranger was any indication of how she would be feeling over the weekend, it was going to be worse than she thought. Drooling over strippers and then going back to a lonely hotel room didn't exactly sound appealing.

She finally managed to make it to the rest of the group. Cindy caught her eye and dropped back until she was walking beside Jessica.

"What happened? I was about to send out search parties. Did you get trapped in a sea of cowboys?" she asked, gesturing toward a nearby bunch of men, all of whom fit the description.

She wasn't that far off.

Jessica said, "I stepped wrong and twisted my ankle. I'm all right," she added quickly, seeing that Cindy was about to take on a mother-hen role, "but I did kind of have a little encounter with a hot guy."

Cindy's expression turned from worried caregiver to giggly teenager in two seconds flat. "Seriously? That's awesome! Did he catch you as you fell, and then you shared a kiss before you rushed off into the crowd, leaving him brokenhearted?"

That sounded way better than what had actually happened. "You watch way too many movies. He just asked if I was okay."

Cindy's face fell a little. Jessica couldn't let her friend look so disappointed. "And then he gave me his phone number."

Cindy stopped dead in her tracks. "Are you kidding? That's *amazing*!"

Jessica could hear the emphasis of the last word. Cindy would probably have written it with five exclamation points. And all of the exclamation points would have little hearts instead of dots. Jessica laughed.

Cindy put a hand on her hip. "I've been telling you to go out on a date for weeks now. Here's your chance! And by date, I absolutely mean crazy sex with a random stranger. We're in Vegas, after all."

Jessica tugged at her friend's sleeve, trying to catch up with Cindy's friends. The other women had just turned a corner, and getting lost in the airport would be a less-than-perfect start to this weekend. "I'm not going to call him, Cindy."

Cindy started walking but kept her eyes firmly fixed on Jessica. "Why not? You have to follow up on this."

"With the stranger who I met for two seconds in an airport in Vegas? That doesn't sound like the start of a lasting relationship."

Cindy was unperturbed. "Who said anything about a lasting relationship? I just want you to hook up with this guy. You are totally allowed to bail on my bachelorette party if you're hooking up with a guy."

Jessica held up a finger. "One—you're just all excited about this because you're happy and in love and therefore like to set people up." She put up a second finger. "And two—this is exactly the kind of situation where the girl ends up going out on a date with a murderer and her friends all say, 'It was so unlike her to go out with total strangers, but we convinced her it would be a good idea and now she's dead.' No, thank you."

Cindy raised one eyebrow, giving her friend her patented "I'm not convinced" look before rolling her eyes. "Fine, come up with all the excuses you want about why you won't call him. You liked what you saw and that terrified you. I get it."

Cindy stopped and crossed her arms, as if waiting for Jessica to take the bait. Jessica knew her friend wanted her to argue with her, but she also had been around Cindy long enough that she didn't need to rise to the occasion and defend her actions. Especially because what she said was probably true.

Jessica shrugged and kept walking, and Cindy had no choice but to keep up.

Together they found the baggage claim area. Everyone but Jessica had brought giant suitcases that needed to be picked up. As they stepped off the last escalator, Jessica spotted a man in a suit with a driver's hat holding a sign that read Mrs. Cynthia Frederickson. She elbowed Cindy. "Looks like you have a chauffeur, Mrs. Frederickson."

Cindy squealed in delight at seeing her future married name. "This is so much fun! I need to have a bachelorette party at least once a year from now on."

Jessica shook her head as Cindy ran over to the man, bewildering him with her enthusiasm. Cindy was unlike anyone else Jessica had ever met, and she loved her for it.

The group of women followed in Cindy's wake, and once again Jessica found herself trailing behind. The chauffer gathered their luggage—no easy feat, since all the bags were giant and seemed very heavy—and led the women outside to the largest and most garish limo Jessica had ever seen. It was basically a very long SUV with flashing LED lights all over it.

The women around her laughed and screeched with pleasure. "I love this city!" Cindy cried in delight.

Miss New York started singing "Viva Las Vegas" and a few others joined in as they hauled themselves up the steps into the back of the outrageous vehicle. Jessica had to laugh at how ridiculous it all was. Normally she would roll her eyes if she saw that monstrosity rolling down the street—and probably make some comment about consumerism or the environment—but for this moment, this weekend, she was just going to go with it.

She ducked into the dark, laughter-filled limo. She was in Las Vegas and was getting on board, both literally and metaphorically.

AARON WEATHERS HEADED toward the private car he'd arranged weeks in advance. Normally it would seem silly to get a private car for a five-minute drive, but he'd learned long ago that the expense was worth it if it meant he didn't have to wait in the soul-crushing taxi line at the airport.

This time, however, he lingered an extra few seconds before getting in, taking one last look while his friend Jeremiah walked around and got in the other side. Maybe he could get another glimpse of the girl from the terminal before he left.

Unfortunately there was a gargantuan SUV limo in the way of the baggage claim area, so he couldn't see much. As it took off, he ducked into the backseat of the town car.

It had been quick, a couple of minutes at the most, that they had stood together, and he wanted to see her again, even if just for a second to make sure she was real. It had been the strangest thing. He'd turned his head and there she was, staring at him with deep green eyes that hooked him somehow. He'd been close enough to see the flecks of gold in them. Her long flowing hair, dark red and curling lightly at the edges, made his fingers ache to slide through it.

Aaron had liked everything about her. The eyes, the hair, the small dusting of freckles, her height. She was taller than most of the men around her, even in her low-heeled boots. Which weren't quite low enough, he thought with a smile.

The moment she had started to fall, he instinctively jumped forward. She had caught herself in time, but if she had actually fallen, he would have been there to save her. In a way, he regretted that it was unnecessary because then perhaps she would feel more reason to call the stranger who had given her his number.

She had left so quickly the story felt incomplete. He had no way of contacting her. He half wished he had run after her, tried to get her name and number, but that seemed like the move a crazy person would make, which wasn't exactly the impression he wanted to leave on her. If there was any possibility she might call, chasing her down would most likely be a deal-breaker. Besides, he couldn't ditch Jeremiah like that.

He wished he'd gotten her name, though.

She intrigued him, and he wanted to see her again. If she didn't get in touch, what chance would he ever have of finding her again? Based on her clothes and the heavy jacket slung over her arm, it was apparent she came from some cold city and he highly doubted she was in town for the rodeo.

What if he never saw her again, and that was all there was to it?

2

AARON LEANED BACK against the supple leather of his seat and pictured the woman from the airport, imagining her walking toward him and giving him a sexy smile. She hadn't given him one, but he knew it was there, hiding, waiting for the right moment. He only pulled out of his reverie when he noticed Jeremiah leaning against the car door and staring at him, his arms crossed.

"What are you thinking about? Did you hear anything I was saying?"

Aaron had been so absorbed in his fantasy he hadn't even realized his friend was talking. After a pause, he admitted, "I—was thinking about this woman I just met in the airport."

"You met a girl? Already? Where was I?"

"It was when we were leaving the gate, so I'm guessing you were still flirting with the flight attendant."

Jeremiah nodded his agreement. "I love flight attendants."

"You have never managed to get one to go out with you. Not once. You know that, right?"

Jeremiah shrugged. "Well, sure, but if I keep trying, one of them is bound to think I'm adorable one of these days."

Jeremiah linked his fingers behind his head and leaned back, completely content in his failure. Even after being friends for pretty much their entire lives, Jeremiah's tenacity and good humor never ceased to amaze Aaron.

After a few seconds of quiet reverie, Jeremiah turned his attention back to Aaron. "So, this girl you met. Hot?"

Aaron nodded. That didn't even begin to describe her.

"Did you set something up with her? Get her name and number?"

If only.

"I managed to give her mine before she took off, but I didn't get hers. I don't think she'll call, though."

Jeremiah shrugged again. "If she calls, great. If she doesn't, no big loss."

He was always so accepting of any situation, Aaron never quite knew if it was admirable or annoying.

Jeremiah continued, "We've been in Vegas for ten minutes and you already found a girl, and she definitely won't be the only beautiful lady you see this weekend. We'll find some chicks that make her look like Mrs. Jessup in comparison, no matter how pretty she was."

Aaron seriously doubted that, but he didn't attempt to explain it. He vividly remembered Mrs. Jessup, their seventh grade teacher, and the woman in the airport would never look anything like that, no matter what supermodel she was standing next to.

He couldn't describe how he felt to his friend, but it wasn't just that the woman from the airport was attractive. She was, but that wasn't all there was to this—this whatever it was. He'd seen plenty of beautiful women in his life, but none of them had struck him the way she did. None of them made his blood light on fire just by looking at him. There was something about the way she carried herself, something about the discerning look in her eyes.

There was no way to say any of that to Jeremiah, and it didn't matter, anyway. She was gone, and there was nothing he could do to make her call him. She had run away so quickly after he gave her his number, and now the moment and the woman had disappeared. Normally he would've been more eloquent, more convincing, but she had made it hard to think straight.

He tried to shift his thinking to focus on the rodeo and the other women he'd meet. He even tried to picture Olivia, who he'd met up with every year and was expecting to see at the big team roping event on Saturday. She was an amazing blonde, voluptuous in all the right places and always willing to spend an evening at his side. But his thoughts kept straying back to the woman from the airport.

The car slid through the airport traffic, passing by the rodeo venue on its way to the hotel. The entire thing was covered in banners with pictures of horses and National Finals Rodeo written everywhere in huge letters. Jeremiah bounced in his seat. "Man, I love rodeo weekend!"

Aaron chuckled. "I know. You've said that about thirty times since we left this morning."

"But it's true! The NFR is awesome. Great events, Vegas, beautiful women everywhere and this year, my team is going to kill it. But mostly the women."

They arrived at the hotel before the two men had even sunk fully into the plush leather seats. They were staying at the Hard Rock Hotel, a mile or so from the airport and within walking distance of the rodeo venue, making it the perfect location.

As taxis full of cowboys headed toward Las Vegas Boulevard, Jeremiah rolled his eyes. "Why does anyone stay on the Strip?"

When Aaron and Jeremiah went to the NFR years ago for the first time as single adults without supervision, they'd stayed in the Bellagio, a grandiose affair, thinking it would put them in the middle of the party. They'd realized quickly that it just put them in the middle of Las Vegas Boulevard traffic. The surroundings didn't make up for the inconvenient distance they had to travel each day, which had to be driven through at a crawl.

They grabbed their bags and walked into the darkened casino.

Hard Rock, though off-Strip, was still iconic and interesting enough for Aaron's taste, and he'd found the suites to be perfectly satisfying, to put it mildly. Walking the short distance with his arm wrapped around a woman's waist and leading her into his room never went wrong.

He couldn't help wondering, though, if the woman he'd seen would be in one of the big hotels on the Strip, and that maybe he should've gotten a room there instead. If she didn't call, at least there would still be a possibility he could spot her again walking through one of the casinos.

Practically rolling his eyes at his own thoughts, he gave himself a mental shake. It was time to stop focusing on this one woman. If she called, she called. He couldn't let something as little as a chance meeting of eyes disrupt his entire weekend, even if picturing her sent a strange new thrill through his chest...and elsewhere.

Aaron promised himself he wouldn't think of her again for the rest of the weekend.

They entered the casino and dodged through tourists and gamblers until they stood in front of the reception desk, where a pretty, young hotel clerk waved them over. Jeremiah leaned in, whispering frantically before they got within earshot of her, "You already got a girl. This one's mine."

Aaron had absolutely no problem with that. Jeremiah was usually the one going for strange women he had zero chance with, not Aaron. Once in a day was enough for him.

Jeremiah rested his arms on the counter, taking up all the space available, leaving Aaron standing behind him, glad to have a good view of what he was sure would be quite the interaction. Jeremiah leaned in slightly toward the clerk, and Aaron could tell he was trying to read her name tag. "Hi, Lucy. How are you on this beautiful evening?"

The woman gave him a polite smile. "Fine, sir. What name is the reservation under?"

"Aaron Weathers," Aaron called over Jeremiah's shoulder.

As usual, he'd reserved both his and Jeremiah's rooms, since his friend hated the idea of paying for a luxury suite and had tried a few times to get them some basic rooms to cut down on costs. Aaron's ranch was working smoothly, his inheritance was well invested and dropping a couple grand on some hotel rooms was worth it if it could give them an amazing weekend.

As the woman typed in the information, Jeremiah tilted his head toward Aaron. "That's my friend. I'm Jeremiah. We're here for the rodeo. Have you ever been to the rodeo?"

"No, sir, I haven't. Mr. Weathers, we have you two down for a suite, is that correct?"

Jeremiah jumped in quickly. "Suites, with an *S*. Two separate suites. We won't be staying together."

Aaron stepped up and slapped his friend on the back. "I think she gets it, Jeremiah," he said as he handed the woman his ID and credit card.

As they left the counter with the key cards, Aaron studied the indomitable Jeremiah. He seemed just as happy as ever, despite being completely dismissed by the pretty clerk. Aaron wondered for the first time if Jeremiah purposely flirted with women he couldn't possibly get.

It was an interesting thought, but he dismissed it. Jeremiah was just so unstoppably optimistic that he had to assume every girl wanted him, despite whatever evidence he was faced with.

They maneuvered through the casino to the elevators and made their way to the top floor. The suite was as spectacular as Aaron remembered, with a private bar area and separate rooms. The Las Vegas Strip shimmered from the huge windows. Jeremiah turned to him. "Okay, so we have about two hours before we need to leave for dinner. The girls are going to meet us there. Quick nap, and then we meet up? If things go according to plan, it's going to be a long night." Jeremiah seemed giddy at the prospect.

Aaron nodded, but couldn't summon his usual enthusiasm, even with Jeremiah practically dancing with excitement. By the time he was in his room, he was so frustrated at his inability to focus his mind away from his airport mystery woman that he simply gave up; he fell asleep imagining her walking up to him, sliding her arm around his neck and pulling him in for a long, deep kiss.

JESSICA LEANED BACK in the limo as it slowly wound through the city. She had assumed they would be heading to the hotel and crashing for the night—after all, it was nearly ten and they'd just gotten off a long flight—but apparently she'd been wrong. They were stopping at the Palazzo, one of the glitzy casinos on the Strip, just long enough to drop off their bags and change, which for the rest of the girls seemed to mean slipping into shorter skirts and higher heels and throwing on some more makeup.

Jessica opened her small bag and looked at her two dresses folded next to her jeans and T-shirts. The jeans looked so comfortable, but she could just imagine Cindy's reaction if she even tried to put them on and grabbed a dress instead. It was a purple lacy thing that went to her knees—she had purchased it for a cousin's summer wedding the year before. It wasn't as comfortable as her jeans but was as close as a dress could get.

As she held it up to see how wrinkled it was, Cindy spoke up behind her. "No. Jessica, you are *not* wearing your purple 'wedding guest' dress. It's not a clubbing dress!"

"I don't have clubbing dresses. You know that," Jessica reminded her friend, hoping Cindy would accept it and let her slip it on.

Cindy gave her a triumphant smile, and Jessica waited for whatever disaster it foreshadowed. Cindy said, "It just so happens that I was very aware of that and took the liberty to pack a few dresses for you. And shoes that match so you don't try to wear those boots or whatever ridiculous shoes you brought."

Jessica almost said something about the difference in what she and Cindy considered to be ridiculous footwear, but she kept her mouth shut. It was her friend's weekend—she could suffer through a few uncomfortable nights. She shrugged. "Whatever you say, boss. It's your weekend."

Cindy's grin widened. "I was really hoping you

would say that. Ladies, Jessica needs help with her hair and makeup. Hurry! We have dinner reservations."

In less than a minute, Jessica found herself sitting on the edge of the hotel room's bathtub, her eyes closed, with Cindy and Alexis or whoever tugging at her hair, the one who was either Marilyn or Arely brushing eye shadow across her eyelids, and somebody else scraping at her lips with a lipstick pencil thing.

"This color is perfect on you," one of them said. Jessica couldn't move her mouth to respond or open her eyes to see who it was.

She had been Cindy's guinea pig enough times to not move unless she wanted a burn from a curling iron or a stab in the eye, so she just stayed still until they moved away, satisfied.

"You look so pretty!" Cindy exclaimed. "And don't you dare tuck your hair behind your ears."

Jessica glanced in the mirror. Actually she *did* look pretty good. Her hair curled over her shoulders in a way it never did for her, and her eyes looked big and greener than usual.

"We need to get going," Cindy called out to the women as they rushed around making last-minute adjustments to themselves.

Jessica had just realized she was still wearing her button-down shirt and yoga pants from the flight when a small red bundle of fabric hit her arm. She looked to see who had thrown it.

Cindy smiled at her. "Put it on and don't complain. We have to go!"

The moment she unrolled the dress, Jessica could

see why Cindy had waited until the last minute to give it to her. "Cindy, this is going to be way too short on me. I can't wear this."

Cindy didn't even turn around. "Don't care. You said I'm the boss. It'll be fun!"

Jessica bit back her grumbling and slid into the dress. Her legs stuck out of it like flagpoles, and if she pulled it down another inch, the top would reveal enough to get her arrested for public indecency. What was Cindy thinking?

But there was nothing to be done. She slipped into the four-inch heels that Cindy had set beside her, a pair Cindy had tried to get her to borrow at least a dozen times and had now finally succeeded in foisting upon her, and left the hotel room without looking in the mirror. She didn't want to know how awkward and gangly she looked.

She felt as if she was towering over everyone else, but there was nothing she could do about it. They were already on their way, off for dinner and clubs and who knew what else?

Before walking out the door, though, she rushed back to her pants and pulled a slip of paper out of the pocket. She folded it carefully and slid it into the tiny purse Cindy had lent her. Not that she would call him, of course. It simply felt better to have it with her. Just in case.

Back in the limousine, Jessica felt like leaning her head against the window, but forced herself to sit upright. It had been a long day, and all the excitement left Jessica feeling worn down, her nerves frayed from the constant chatter. And it had hardly begun.

But she was determined to stay optimistic. It could end up being a fun evening if she managed to stay awake past her ten-thirty bedtime. Besides, there was a possibility she could meet Aaron the cowboy again, magically solving her dilemma about whether or not to call him. It wasn't too far beyond the realm of reason, and even if it was, a girl could dream, couldn't she?

Jessica would have slapped her own forehead in annoyance if she was sure Cindy wouldn't yell at her for messing with her makeup.

Jessica watched as Cindy and her friends danced to the loud music thumping through the speakers she had somehow managed to block out—it was some song she'd never heard but they all seemed to know—and they were laughing and shouting unintelligibly at each other.

She smiled at them, glad they were enjoying themselves, but she couldn't help feeling incredibly out of place. Again.

It would take a lot of liquor to get her even half as comfortable and free as these women were at the moment, despite being stone sober. Why couldn't she just let loose and dance and giggle like them?

It was as if she were a scientific observer watching a unique species and trying to understand them. She was near the women, but that didn't make her one of them.

Luckily nobody seemed to notice that she wasn't bumping along, so she kept that smile plastered on her face and tried to look as though she was enjoying herself.

"We're here!" Cindy suddenly called out.

Their first stop was Firefly, a Spanish tapas restaurant off Las Vegas Boulevard. Jessica took a deep breath, trying to clear out the crazy idea that she would somehow spot Aaron here.

If she didn't let that idea go, it was going to spoil her whole weekend. She could either call him or not, but thinking random chance would throw them together was beyond idiotic.

She walked down the steps of the SUV limo carefully, very aware that another near spill like in the airport when this high up would probably end with a trip to the hospital. She wasn't exactly confident in the heels she was wearing, and was relieved and quite proud of herself when her feet were on asphalt.

Marilyn/Arely—their names were *way* too similar—followed her out and took a deep breath. "Don't you love Vegas? This is their December weather!"

Jessica couldn't agree more. The night air was cool, but not cold enough to cause discomfort despite the thin fabric of her dress, and the air smelled deliciously of spices and seafood. Vegas had a few things going for it, that was for sure. Early December in New York involved biting winds and the musty smell of melting snow mixed in with the garbage. This was much better.

Once all the women successfully climbed out of their outlandish vehicle, they strolled into the restaurant as one mass of femininity. They were seated at a private booth, and several waiters descended on them.

"Hello, ladies," one began as the other placed pitchers of sangria on the table. "Welcome to Firefly. We will bring out a variety of tapas for you to enjoy once you are settled. Please enjoy your meal and let us know if there is anything we can do to make your evening more pleasant."

Cindy had told Jessica that the first night's dinner was all part of whatever package her sorority sisters had picked out for her, but she'd had no idea it would be quite like this. Within minutes, dozens of plates filled with bite-size delicious morsels were spread across the table and her glass was filled with sangria, fruit floating around in it cheerfully. How much had the sorority sisters spent on this? She felt bad for Lacy, the one who had been unable to come and whose place she was currently filling.

These girls all seemed to really love Cindy.

The alcohol was a welcome addition to the evening, and Jessica drank a large glassful to steady herself and throw off her discomfort, and then another to try and help her forget the blue eyes that kept swimming to the front of her consciousness.

By the time they left, she was full and had downed enough sangria to help the next hour or two pass in a blur. She even danced with the other women at some very dark, very loud nightclub. She laughed and shouted with them, just one of the girls. This wasn't college anymore, where she'd been too tall and awkward, too much of a homebody to let loose like this.

As they made it to their last stop of the evening, however, the alcohol was wearing off and she'd begun to get back to her old self, and her old self was very uncomfortable with the fact that she was walking into a strip club.

She would have fun, though. How bad could it be?

As she was ushered along into the side of the Sapphire Club designated for female clientele, her mind began to recoil at the mostly nude women leading the way to the other section of the club. Not because they were nearly naked—that could've been even a bit exciting if her drinks weren't wearing off. It was because they were not the sexy alluring women she'd expected. Instead they looked like any other bored women stuck at work. With the exception of their clothing, of course.

The men were worse. They were handsome, to an extent, and all had some pretty impressive abs, but as soon as the show began, Jessica knew she was not where she wanted to be. Something about it bothered her, and though she knew it was supposed to be fun to ogle the strippers, she just couldn't bring herself to do it.

After a few minutes, she made a decision. She walked over to Cindy, who was surrounded by giggling friends and dancing men in their underwear. Leaning in to her friend's ear, Jessica pressed on Cindy's arm to get her attention. "I'm going outside for some fresh air. It's okay, I'm having fun," she continued quickly, seeing that her friend was about to scold. "I just need to take a walk. Enjoy yourself and I'll see you in a little bit!"

She smiled as she walked away to show Cindy that everything was fine, then turned around and got out of there as quickly as she could.

Outside, the air was fresh and clean. She took deep breaths of it, enjoying the sensation as it ran through her, just cold enough to tickle her lungs. She moved away from the door and began strolling, slightly unsteadily in her too-tall shoes, around the parking lot. She considered taking them off and walking barefoot, but she didn't want to even imagine what kind of diseases she could catch if she stepped on something.

She was a little disappointed in herself at first, thinking she should have stuck it out and tried to enjoy the show.

When she thought about it, though, she knew it wouldn't have worked. All the other women seemed to think those men grinding against them was fantastic, but it just wasn't in her nature. She was only attracted to guys who were intelligent, never wasting time drooling over handsome men she didn't know.

Well, except for the one.

Jessica pulled the folded paper from her purse, looking again at the blocky writing. She wanted to tell herself that he *seemed* smart, though she had no idea how she could've decided that in the few seconds of their interaction—he'd used a bookmark to give her his number, after all. Not that she had any idea what book it had been, but it seemed thick enough to be important and literary.

It seemed much more likely that she was just as shallow as everyone else and swooned the moment she saw a sexy cowboy. That had to be all it was, which was a relief, in a way, because that would make him easier to forget.

Jessica kept walking, considering for the thousandth time whether or not to call him. Then she had the urge to call her family and check on them, at least as a way to occupy her mind and stop herself from doing something incredibly foolish. But it was past four in the morning in New York, far too late at night to call without a very good reason.

Her mom would kill her if she called that late, but it didn't stop Jessica from wanting to feel near them. Since her father's diagnosis a year ago, she had seen her family nearly every day, and even if it was a burden sometimes, the distance now clawed at her nerves.

Not being around for four days, not helping with medicine, driving to the doctor visits and helping her mom and sister seemed an impossibly long time. What if something happened? She hadn't been away more than two days at a time in the past year, and his six months to live had come and gone. He was still battling away, but she knew what could happen.

When Jessica was asked to take Lacy's place on the Vegas trip, her father was the one who did most of the convincing. He had squeezed her hand and said, "You need a vacation. Enjoy yourself for a few days just this once."

And now here she was, wandering through a strip club parking lot in the early hours of the morning. She doubted this was what he'd had in mind.

Jessica finished her circuit of the lot and was beginning another when a small mob of people stumbled out of the entrance, laughing loudly and chattering at the top of their lungs. They had to be absolutely smashed. She glanced at the party to see if any of Cindy's friends needed to be rescued, but none of them were in the group. There was someone she *did* recognize, though, and the sight stopped her in her tracks. She couldn't have been more shocked if someone walked up and slapped her in the face.

It was him. Straight out of her fairy tale and back into the real world, only not like her fairy tale at all. Aaron.

At first she couldn't believe it, but it was definitely Aaron from the airport. The same man, this time with his muscular arms wrapped around two women who were wearing little more than the strippers, and he was laughing and joking while staring down the too-low top of the girl on his right.

3

APPARENTLY HER IMAGINED version of him was not quite true to life.

Judging by the cowboy's ogling, he wasn't the kind of guy to walk up and whisper words of love unless they were helping him get into a woman's pants. It seemed pretty clear that he hadn't given her his number because of some special magical connection. He just saw a girl who was obviously attracted to him and he thought she'd be an easy lay.

If only her body would get the message and stop tingling.

She had pictured seeing him again in some strange happenstance, only now that it had happened, she was forced to abandon her fantasy world for harsh reality.

That was when Jessica realized she was standing in a pool of light from a streetlamp and staring bug-eyed at the group, and that he'd notice her any second if she didn't do something about it. She turned away, looking desperately for a place to hide before she was spotted.

"Hey! Airport girl!"

Too late.

She abandoned her attempt to retreat and turned back toward the strip club and her drunk fantasy man, trying to throw as much scorn into her expression as she could to hide her embarrassment. He had been so attractive, was still so attractive, but now she knew exactly what kind of man he was. Not the kind she'd ever waste her time on.

Still, her heart betrayed her, jumping at the fact that he recognized her so quickly, as if she *was* special. What a dumb thought. She had misjudged the situation, that was all, and she was annoyed at herself for her lack of insight. Being annoyed was much better than being hurt—there was no reason she should feel hurt, anyway.

"Airport girl! It's you!"

"My name's Jessica, *not* Airport Girl," she responded, hoping he would hear the tone in her voice and back off.

She wasn't going to give this guy an opportunity to make her suffer, despite the attraction she felt for him. At least *this* time she could see the semitruck of heartbreak coming a mile away and could get out of the way before she got flattened.

"Jessica! That's your name! Great. You want to go for a drink?"

His words slurred together a bit when he spoke, but she was able to figure out what he was saying. "It seems like you've probably had enough," she stated coldly as he stumbled toward her.

When he closed the gap between them, she backed

up until she was pressing her shoulder blade into the light pole behind her. He leaned forward, putting his arm on the metal post and leaving only a gap of inches between her face and his. She could smell the alcohol on his breath, but she could also smell his cologne and the musky odor of his skin. The nerves in her fingers fired sensations through her. He was so near and her breath hitched as she imagined herself pressing herself against him, fusing her body with his, lips meeting. Warmth pooled low in her belly.

But her brain managed to stop her, pressing the panic button until the rest of her paid attention. This man was far too close to her and she needed to get away from him, regardless of how enticing the other option might be.

He leaned in another half inch and stared directly into her eyes, and she couldn't help looking back. The warm blue had turned dark from desire, and his voice was pitched soft and low when he spoke, rumbling through her like shock waves. "Do you want to go to my room?"

Yes! her body screamed out. *No! Run!* Her brain shouted back. Lucky for her sanity, he didn't move any closer.

After a deep, shuddering breath, she managed to sidestep out from under his powerful presence and get herself into clear space. As she did so, some other guy who was standing with the women near the front of the club called out, "Aaron, let's go! I don't want to stand here all night, and neither do these lovely ladies," as he leaned over to one and kissed her on the cheek.

One of the girls joined in, beckoning to Aaron as if she were getting a German shepherd to heel. "Come on!"

It was very clear to Jessica that her stranger had plenty of company for the evening already. With as much force as she could muster, she said, "You need to leave me alone. Go back to your friends."

And she spun away from him, marching toward the waiting limo.

As she stormed toward the vehicle and climbed in, her head was a flurry of thoughts, and she couldn't stop them from rushing one after another. *What an idiot. God, he smelled amazing. Another asshole. I should've known. I swear, I hate men. I wish my hands would stop tingling like that. Why do I only seem to like terrible men? He had amazing arms. Maybe I should have kissed him. No, that would've been the worst thing I have ever done. Dammit, I'm crying. I hope he didn't see that.*

As soon as she was safely hidden away from peering eyes with the door closed, Jessica allowed a few tears to slip down her cheeks. She wasn't sure exactly why she was crying over a man she didn't even know, a lost opportunity that had never been an opportunity at all. She just felt very, very alone.

Jessica wiped at her face, only to notice she had something in her hand. It was the paper Aaron had given her a few hours before, his phone number. She had taken it out while she was walking, wondering whether or not she should call him. But that was before she knew the kind of person he was.

Jessica stared at it for a moment—how could she have been so stupid as to even consider calling the number of a complete stranger?—and then crumpled it in her fist and threw it into the tiny trash can beneath the limo's bar.

After a few minutes of quiet weeping, she wiped her eyes on the corner of her dress. She had to hike it up above her waist to do so and left makeup smudges on the hemline, but it made her face look a little more presentable when she looked at her reflection in the window. She shifted her gaze to the dark street and empty parking lot beyond the glass. The group was gone. Aaron was gone.

She curled against the cushions of the spacious interior and closed her eyes, exhausted from the day.

THE SOUND OF the door opening woke her, and the rest of the bachelorette party filed in, loud and raucous and discussing the different men they'd ogled.

A few were giggling like schoolgirls about "the other side of the club," the part with the female strippers, and the customers over there who had bought them drinks and flirted.

"Marilyn even got a phone number from some random guy!" the black-haired one—Anna, her name was Anna—gushed.

Marilyn shrugged, as if this was an everyday occurrence. "Did you see how hot he was? Of course I got his number. I'm going to call him tomorrow and get him to hang out with us. I even like his name. Jeremiah. It rolls nicely off the tongue. I probably would have taken him back to the room tonight if he hadn't disappeared when we went back to check on Cindy."

Jessica turned her attention to her friend, whose head was resting on her knees. Jessica had never seen her that drunk. From the way the other girls looked at her, a mixture of amusement and pity, it was clear she'd spent a decent amount of time throwing up in the bathroom.

Jessica squeezed Cindy's hand, but her friend was already half-asleep.

The conversations washed over Jessica as she attempted to listen and be a part of the group. She was still groggy from sangria and sleep, still feeling gloomy, and she wanted nothing more than to curl up in bed. Thankfully the limousine started to pull away from the strip club and turned toward the hotel.

She grabbed her phone and turned on the screen, the bright light stinging her eyes. It was nearly four in the morning.

AARON LOOKED AT the clock on the bedside table of his suite, and four o'clock glared back at him. But he wasn't feeling tired. He felt sick and annoyed at himself. The room was dark, the large bed unpleasantly empty. He went back through his choices of the evening, unable to get over the level of idiocy.

After sleeping for a couple of hours and getting ready, he and Jeremiah had headed out to dinner at Bouchon, one of the top restaurants in Vegas, where they were joined by a few "friends" they'd met in Vegas in the past few years. He and Jeremiah had organized this dinner weeks before, trying to get their long weekend started off right, but once they'd arrived, Aaron's heart hadn't been in it.

The women were gorgeous and throwing themselves at him, and they had grown up on farms and ranches as he did. All the things that would normally have made his evening buzz with excitement, but he just couldn't stay interested. Much of the meal was spent picturing his mystery girl, then trying to figure out what the people around him had said, usually responding with a very clever "Hmm."

He kept looking around for her, even though the likelihood of seeing her again was so minuscule. A scan of the room, then the realization that Jeremiah and the girls were waiting for an answer from him. "Hmm."

It was not going well.

With nothing better to do, and to try to help him focus on the moment at hand, he drank more ridiculously priced whiskey than he would normally allow himself.

He kept checking his phone, on the off chance the woman had called or messaged him, but there was nothing.

After dinner, thoroughly smashed, he had followed Jeremiah and the women, none of whom were much more sober than he was, to a club. Then Jeremiah, his eyes glinting, said, "I have an idea…"

Things were fuzzy there—he was pretty sure he'd called his voice mail just in case he had gotten a call—but during that time, his friend had somehow talked the girls into going to a strip club. Something had been said about being in Vegas, after all.

By the time they'd gotten to Sapphire, Aaron was starting to feel sober again, and he wasn't happy about it. He'd been to strip clubs before—he was a guy, and a friend of Jeremiah's. It came with the territory.

But he'd never really seen the appeal, in truth. If he wanted a naked woman rubbing against him, he preferred not to be paying her.

This time, though, he couldn't even pretend he wanted to be there, but he didn't want to be alone in his suite, either. And for some stupid reason he couldn't get his fantasy of the airport girl out of his head enough to want to be back at his hotel with the women standing around him, even though they seemed more than willing to keep him company.

While Jeremiah had a great time staring at the women on the stage and flirting with any female in his vicinity, Aaron sat at the bar and had another drink. And another.

When Jeremiah and his entourage of women came to get Aaron so they could leave, he was unsteady on his feet and his mouth had felt too unwieldy to form words properly. Two ladies, both of whom he'd spent nights with other rodeo weekends, pulled his arms around their shoulders and led him out, laughing and chatting.

He had tried to join in but was captivated by the voluptuous and prominently displayed breasts of the woman on his left. He thought she was named Laura, but he had trouble focusing enough to be sure. In his state, he couldn't help staring, and as he did so, he wondered what the airport girl's breasts looked like. He'd bet they were beautiful.

That was when he looked up, and there she was, as if materialized from his fantasy. She was turning away from him and several yards away, but even then he could see that the dress she was wearing revealed the tops of the luscious breasts he'd just been imagining, and the short skirt and tall heels showed off her impossibly long legs. Even drunk, he was clearheaded enough to see that shifting the dress just a few inches in either direction would serve up some amazing views.

If he'd been sober, he would've tried to be a little more suave, though with the way she made the bottom drop out of his stomach, he wasn't so sure it would have worked, anyway. He might have sounded like a blathering idiot when attempting to talk to her at the best of times, but the alcohol made it worse. Worse than he could have imagined.

He sat up in the giant bed, turned the light on and pressed the heels of his hands into his eyes until it hurt. The pain was a welcome relief; it distracted him from his thoughts and how awful the entire evening had gone.

It seemed pretty certain that she wouldn't be calling him. His stupid choices made any chance of him getting her into his bed impossible. He wanted her like crazy, and he maybe even had a chance at her, and he'd blown it.

She'd stormed away from him, and she might have even been crying. That didn't make any sense, though. He'd been an ass, but could it have been awful enough to make her cry? The thought made his stomach twist unpleasantly.

After she left, he'd been so irritated at himself and

everyone who had dragged him around all evening that he took a separate cab back to the hotel, leaving Jeremiah to deal with the women whatever way he wanted. They had protested when he left, but he just told them he wasn't feeling well and got out of there as quickly as he could.

The ride to the hotel had been a blur of lights and frustration, and he had rushed up to his room as quickly as he could, only to sit there, alone in the dark, and replay the evening over again. Not only had he not forgotten about the woman from the airport; he had screwed things up with her, quite possibly with his best friend, and with a couple of other women he normally would have loved to have alone in a room with him.

What a start to the weekend.

He sighed and shook his head, but that only made him feel nauseated. The alcohol hadn't worn off yet, but he was sober enough to realize that he was in for an ugly morning.

He turned off the light and lay back again, trying unsuccessfully to coax his mind into quieting enough for sleep.

After hours of tossing around on the bed, he finally got up and opened the shades, revealing the floor-to-ceiling window that took up an entire wall of the room. The bright sunlight of the morning was blinding, but his view of Las Vegas, with the desert mountains as a backdrop to the iconic cityscape, was beautiful. He sat on the wide leather couch in his boxers, his feet up on the elegant glass coffee table, and stared out at the majesty of it all.

It was a new day, and he was going to stop the nonsense from the night before and get himself back to normal. After a few minutes of looking at the view, he felt a little more serene, though his dissatisfaction from the previous night was still roiling inside him.

He and Jeremiah were supposed to meet up with their teams at two in preparation for the evening's events, which meant he had a few hours to get himself back to some semblance of normal. Aaron could miss it if he wanted, since there wasn't much for him to do, but he knew Jeremiah thought it was important, and Aaron wanted to support his friend.

If Jeremiah wasn't too pissed at him for abandoning him and being a jackass, of course.

He had to get some air if he was going to make it through the day. Throwing on some workout clothes and running a few miles wouldn't make up for tossing and turning alone all night instead of sleeping curled around the luscious redhead, but it was the best he could think of to get his head right.

Working on his ranch was plenty of exercise, but he had found that running was a great way to clear his head and improve his mood, so he usually ended up going out for a jog several days a week. It was the one thing that might get him back on track.

He hated running on treadmills, so he bypassed the hotel's gym and instead made his way through the casino, heading for the exit. After stepping out the front door and into the mild sunshine of winter in Vegas, he turned toward the Strip, figuring it would be more pedestrian friendly than regular streets.

As he jogged, the fresh air against his cheeks and his shoes slapping against the pavement, he started to feel better. By the time he made it to the Flamingo Hotel, he felt halfway normal, and most of the nausea and headache had dissipated.

Aaron continued on his way north, passing several ornate casinos, finally making it to the Venetian and Palazzo hotels. He decided to run a little farther before heading back the way he had come. There were a surprising number of tourists on the streets despite the fact that it was early for vacationers to be up, not even ten, but he managed to move through them without breaking pace.

JESSICA STOOD OUTSIDE the Venetian, leaning against the railing of one of the bridges that arched over the fake canal running in front of the casino doors. As she looked around and soaked in the oddity of the oasis in the middle of the desert and the pedestrians walking by with large Eiffel Tower–shaped alcoholic drinks at barely ten in the morning, she saw a man jog past and instantly realized who it was. The shock and thrill of seeing Aaron once again, this time in basketball shorts and with only a thin white T-shirt on, ran through her body like a jolt of adrenaline.

It had been so difficult to get him off her mind all morning that she wondered if she had somehow deluded herself into thinking it was him, but no. It was definitely the man who had been starring in her imagination since their encounter at the airport.

Before she could do anything stupid like call out to

him, he was out of sight, hidden by people and the decorative hedges that lined the Venetian's walkway. The breath she dragged in shakily after he was gone felt like ice in her lungs, despite the relative warmth of the air.

She bit the inside of her lip, frustrated at her reaction. She knew that she would never feel his body tight against hers, so why did she torture herself with images of him? Erotic thoughts flooded her, but that was enough in itself to make her keep her distance. Trying to start a relationship with this guy would only leave her sitting on a plane home, frustrated with herself for making a choice she knew was bad before it even happened.

There was another option, though. She'd never truly considered having a fling—it wasn't in her nature—but that didn't mean she couldn't. She was always careful around men, distant, thoughtful. In fact, she hadn't admitted it to anyone but Cindy, but Russ had been her first and only, and that was only after months and months of dating.

Still, that didn't mean that she couldn't let go once and enjoy herself without it meaning anything more. Women had no-strings-attached sex all the time. It was the twenty-first century. She could do that.

Hell, maybe it'd be good for her. She had spent so much time anxious about her dad or unhappy about her failed relationship that perhaps a little time feeling sexy and passionate for once in her life would be a welcome change of pace. She didn't *need* to be methodical and sensible all the time.

Except she had thrown out Aaron's number, so even if she decided to change her stripes and enjoy a wild night with an irresponsible man, she had no way to contact the particular man who sent fire through her veins. She was never going to see him again. Even with how crappy she had felt the night before, the loss of the possibility made her sad.

Throughout her musings, she continued to stare at the place where he'd disappeared. When he ran into view again going the opposite direction—as she'd secretly hoped he might—she allowed herself to bask in her attraction, knowing she was safely hidden from his eyes by the crowd.

As he disappeared from view yet again, she came to a decision: if she ever saw him again, she'd consider it a sign and think about doing something about those feelings and being deliciously illogical for a change. As it was, she would let herself fantasize about him, guilt free. She leaned against the railing for a few more minutes before turning around and heading back into the casino, laughing at her agreement with herself.

As if there was any chance she'd ever see him again.

ONCE AARON MADE it back to the hotel, he jumped into the shower for a long, hot rinse to help clear his head. As the water splashed over his skin, his mind wandered once again to his fantasy woman, now with her name attached. He pictured Jessica, and what it would be like to touch her smooth skin, share a shower with her, rubbing her slick body, his hands in her long dark hair. He let himself revel in the scene. He'd have to content himself with his imagination, since the real thing was long gone.

After his shower, he ate and dressed in his jeans, a blue button-down shirt and his cowboy hat, the perfect attire for a day at the rodeo. It was the reason he was in Vegas, after all. By that time, he felt decent enough to try and fix a few of his mistakes from the night before, starting with Jeremiah.

As for Jessica, he doubted he would ever see her again, but if the universe aligned somehow, he wouldn't mess it up. A third chance seemed impossible, but he would definitely keep watch for her.

He thought ahead through his day. It seemed unlikely she would be at the rodeo, but maybe he would get lucky. Then he thought of the women he was sure to run into during the day's events, and he balked at the idea of spending his time with them.

How long had it been since he actually enjoyed the company of any of those buckle bunnies? Why had he thought hooking up with them was so great, and when had he stopped feeling that way?

He'd never before felt that fire and heat course through him the way it had done when he was just *looking* at Jessica.

He repeated her name to himself: *Jessica.* Anything less than that sensation seemed pointless when he knew that it was out there.

Even if he never met her again, maybe he'd find that feeling somewhere else, though he wasn't sure about that. He'd never seen eyes like hers before. Or legs.

He needed help.

He heard his phone buzz, bringing him back to reality. Vegas was not the place to start rethinking your outlook on life. Aaron picked it up and glanced at the screen.

Jeremiah had texted Hey. Come over whenever you're ready to go.

Aaron felt a little uncertain about going over to his friend's suite. Would he be pissed about him disappearing the night before?

He tapped out a quick I'll be right over, put on his boots and walked down the hall to the next suite.

As soon as he knocked, his friend opened the door, smiling the widest smile Aaron had ever seen. Jeremiah had barely waved him in before he began telling the story of his night. "Man, last night was awesome! Sorry you weren't feeling great. You really missed out. Those two hanging all over you were pretty disappointed. I bet you could've gotten both of them. You hear what I'm saying? *Both* of them.

"Anyway, I dropped them off at the Bellagio on the way back here. You know Vanessa, right? The brunette with really short hair. She came back here with me. Just left a few minutes ago. You wouldn't believe what happened if I told you. Are you feeling better? You must be hungover like crazy."

Aaron barely had time to register what his friend was saying as Jeremiah wandered around the room, picking up his scattered clothing and gesturing wildly. Aaron was relieved his behavior hadn't bothered Jeremiah. In fact, Jeremiah hadn't seemed to register anything odd about his conversation with Jessica or any of the events of last night.

Aaron said, "Yeah, I felt pretty awful this morning, but I'm better now."

It was somewhat true—he no longer felt like throwing up, at least.

Jeremiah snatched up his phone and room key card and walked back to Aaron, who was still standing near the door. Aaron considered trying to say something to Jeremiah about the night before, but decided against it. No point bringing him down.

As they exited the room, Jeremiah started talking again, giving Aaron even more reason to keep his mouth shut. "Tonight we're having dinner with a bachelorette party, by the way. I met this sexy chick at the strip club who was there with a big group of them, but I managed to pull her aside and get her number. Her name was Marlene. No, that wasn't it. Marilyn. Anyway, there are, like, seven of them besides the bride, and the ones I saw were all crazy hot. They're from back East and in town for a long weekend, so I'm thinking we can get one of them to break away from the pack for you. Marilyn was all over me, so I think I won't have a problem there—"

Jeremiah seemed so proud of himself and excited at the prospect that Aaron nodded, even though the last thing he felt like doing was trying to seduce a strange woman who was probably depressed because her friend was getting married and she was still single. He'd done it before, but it had left him feeling guilty, though the women hadn't seemed to mind. It wasn't as if he told them he was looking for a long-term relationship or anything; it just felt as though he was taking advantage.

Even if he had no qualms about the situation normally, it certainly would not be top of his list this weekend. He still felt terrible about Jessica, and he hadn't forgotten how his heart pounded when he looked at her. He doubted any random woman from a bachelorette party could top that.

Still, there was nothing to be done except go along with his friend, be a good wingman and try to get out of it without hurting anyone's feelings.

He was sure he'd be spending another evening in his hotel bed alone.

4

JESSICA SAT DOWN to lunch at their large reserved table. She was there before the rest of the party and had to force herself not to lean on her hand and fall asleep while she waited. She had assumed she would feel pretty crappy by the end of the wild bachelorette party weekend, but here it was, only Friday. They had been in town a little over twelve hours and she was well on her way to being wiped out.

She couldn't get the sight of Aaron out of her mind and kept replaying the scene from the night before. Sometimes her imaginary self pressed against Aaron and let her hormones take over, letting her hands slide along his muscular arms and across his imagined abs. Those fantasies were the worst because they made every inch of her come alive and set firecrackers off along her spine, and that was the last thing she wanted to happen.

She needed to distract herself somehow, or she would go crazy waiting for the rest of the women. Even though she knew she would get flack for it, Jessica pulled out her phone and called her mom despite the explicit instructions not to do that while she was in Vegas. After the third ring, her mother answered. The first thing Jessica heard was a sigh. "Why are you calling? You should be having fun."

Jessica could hear the love even in her mother's rebuff, and it soothed her soul a little. "I missed my family. Is that so terrible?"

Another sigh. "We saw you less than a day ago. I should've just let it go to voice mail."

Jessica smiled to herself. "You'd never do that to your favorite daughter."

"I'll be telling your sister you said that."

"She knows it's true. Can I talk to Dad?"

There was a brief silence, a quick clearing of a throat, and then her father's voice drifted into her ear. Just hearing him quieted her mind. "What's going on, Jess?"

She shrugged, even though he couldn't see her. "I just wanted to check on the family. See how things are going."

"Not much has changed since yesterday, Jess. I'm fine. Go do something Vegas-y."

"I don't know what that means. Like date a stripper? Gamble away my life savings on craps?"

His laugh, soft but still his own, came pouring out of the phone pressed to her ear. He said, "I was thinking more along the lines of walking around on the Strip or going to see a show, but those are good ideas, too. Stop bothering us and go have a good time."

It was amazing how just a few words from him made her feel so much better. As the rest of her lunch group appeared outside the window, Jessica took a deep breath, ready to face them. "You know you miss me, Dad. Fine, I'll go be Vegas-y. Love you."

"Love you, too. Have fun with your stripper."

Anna, the black-haired one whose name she had finally memorized, walked into the restaurant with the pack of sorority sisters trailing behind her. Each woman looked immaculate, with a wide lipsticked smile. Anna sat next to her, and Jessica slid her phone into her purse. "Hi, Jessica. Wasn't last night so much fun?" Anna asked, full of enthusiasm.

It wasn't exactly the phrase Jessica would use, but Anna seemed sincere, so she just smiled back and answered, "It was definitely a night I'll remember the rest of my life."

She wasn't sure if she had managed to keep the sarcasm out of her voice, but the other women surrounding her all seemed satisfied, nodding in agreement, so she must have done a decent job. They all started reminiscing about the night before as if it were something that had happened years ago instead of a few hours ago.

"That food was so good. If I ate like that every day, I would end up weighing two hundred pounds," said a size-zero pixie. Jessica was pretty sure her name was Destiny.

"What about those guys we danced with at XS?" asked…Mandy? Mindy?…as she nudged Alana?—yeah, definitely Alana.

Definitely-Alana covered her face with her hands, laughing. "You almost got us kicked out of the club, Amanda. I didn't even know that was possible."

Anna, Alana, Amanda. There was an Alexis in here somewhere, too. Why did Cindy need to have so many friends whose names started with A? It was as if she was *trying* to make it confusing. Jessica's head spun as she tried to keep the names straight. Their perkiness and perfection didn't help her mood any.

The only person who looked even remotely as bad as Jessica felt was Cindy, whose face was still slightly green. Even from across the table, Jessica could see the circles under her friend's eyes. She made a mental note to mother her a little whenever they were free of the sea of sorority sisters.

Not that she looked much better despite her more sober and less vomit-worthy morning. She had cringed when she saw herself in the bathroom mirror that morning.

At lunch, she allowed herself to drift in and out of the conversations around her, imagining Aaron in a variety of scenarios, each one as unrealistic as the one before. She hadn't really thought about it before, but it had been far too long since she was with a man. And since she was picturing no ordinary man, it should have come as no surprise that her body was unrelenting in its yearning.

"So, tonight's plan," began Marilyn, quieting the others. "Jeremiah and his friend will be meeting us for dinner at eight-thirty. The limo should be here around eleven, which means plenty of time to eat and drink and gamble. The driver has the details for the clubs we'll hit tonight. Is everyone good with that? Cindy, are you going to survive another night?"

Cindy nodded and attempted a smile. "I should be over my hangover enough by then. If not, I'll just drown it in more alcohol."

This tactic was met with approval by the other women at the table.

Jessica couldn't say she was looking forward to another evening of all this—she was still reeling from the previous night—but she smiled at Cindy and pretended she was excited. She was going to try to have fun with the girls regardless of her natural inclinations. She'd promised herself, for Cindy's sake, to give it a shot.

If nothing else, she could at least sit back and picture Aaron, sweaty from his run, standing close to her and pulling off the T-shirt to expose the muscled stomach and sculpted chest she knew were beneath his clothing. She could smell him again, that heavy scent of his skin. She was happy with her decision to stop fighting the inevitable and let herself enjoy the fantasy, as long as she reminded herself that it wasn't real and never would be.

As the group finished eating and Jessica paid her portion of the astronomical bill—how could a Caesar salad be so expensive?—she squeezed around and between the rest of the group until she was walking next to Cindy. Her friend seemed a little better after the meal, but still had an unhealthy tint to her cheeks. Jessica wrapped her arm around Cindy's shoulders.

"You doing okay?" she asked.

Cindy shrugged and rubbed her face with her hands as they stepped into the elevator to take them to their floor. "I haven't thrown up my soup yet, so that's a good sign. Why did I drink so much?"

Jessica squeezed Cindy's shoulders. "Because you're getting married in two weeks and you're in Vegas. You'll rally tonight. And if you don't want to go out, you don't have to. It's *your* party, you know."

"Don't try to get out of having fun, Jess."

Jessica looked at her friend with wide, innocent eyes as they left the elevator and began walking toward Cindy's room. "I'm not trying to get out of anything. I'm just looking out for your health."

Cindy raised one eyebrow and stared at Jessica. It was clear she didn't buy it. Jessica chuckled. "Okay, okay. We'll have fun tonight. I'll rally, too. I'm just not used to staying up so late."

Cindy stopped in the middle of the hallway and grasped Jessica to her so hard, it almost made Jessica want to cry, though she was unsure why. Her friend said, "I'm glad you came. I know it's not your thing, but thanks for doing it anyways."

Jessica hugged her back. "I'm happy for you, Cindy. Really."

She meant it, too. Sure, it felt a little crappy to watch her roommate's blissful fairy tale when her own romantic track record fell far short of stellar—and trying to find another apartment in New York City had so far been a complete and utter failure—but Cindy was a good person and deserved to be with a guy who loved her.

They broke apart, and Jessica felt better than she had the entire trip. Cindy fumbled through her bag for the key card to her room. "I'm going to take a nap. You should do the same. See you back here in a few hours?"

Jessica nodded. She suddenly felt completely wiped. Perhaps she'd actually be able to sleep a little before she was due back for dinner preparations.

She went back to her room and managed to crash for a couple of hours before getting some work done. Now that she wasn't fighting her mind's insistence on imagining Aaron, it seemed to free up enough mental space to let her behave like a normal human being, which was definitely an improvement. If she could keep pace with her editing workload, she might just be able to turn her temporary job into something serious, and with how expensive it was going to be to rent her own place, if she ever found one, she'd definitely need the money.

At six, Jessica closed her laptop and made her way across the hall to Cindy's room. Although their dinner reservations were still two hours away and at a restaurant just downstairs, she'd been told to come over early to "get ready." She tried not to dread whatever that meant. She wasn't sure she'd be able to survive another of Cindy's chosen outfits.

The moment Jessica walked through the door, it became clear that the night before was only a small example of what these women wanted to do to her. Everyone turned as she came in, smiling in anticipation. A chair had been moved into the bathroom hallway, and every available surface was spread with more beauty products than she could count. Lip and eye pencils were lined up like surgeon's tools.

Cindy, looking much better than she had before, pointed to the chair. "Sit. We've got a plan."

There was nothing to do but sit.

As Alana and Destiny pounced on her, starting with her fingernails and her hair, the other women examined her like artists studying a blank canvas.

Marilyn said, "We have two hours. Hair will take a half hour, easy. An hour if we try to put it up."

Alexis broke in. "We can try it up, but I really think it's prettier down."

"Well, let's curl first and see how a couple of things look. We can always take it back down."

The others agreed. Jessica stayed quiet in her seat, letting the experts talk. She assumed they didn't mean a ponytail when they talking about putting it "up," so they were already beyond her skills.

Amanda tilted Jessica's chin so she was staring into the overhead light. Two thoughts went through Jessica's head. First, she was impressed that she had learned most of their names. Second, she wondered at what point she had started to feel comfortable around these women. She wasn't ecstatic about being a dress-up doll, but she liked the people surrounding her and was happy they were enjoying the weekend.

Amanda said, "We should get foundation and mascara done now, but wait for the rest until a half hour before we go so it won't smudge."

Now that they had a plan, the group broke into teams, some fussing with her hair, others working on their own preparations and still others having conversations while they waited for their turn at the mirror. It was a cacophony of noise and movement, and though Jessica didn't feel like a part of it, she knew she wasn't exactly an outsider any longer, either.

"Who wants drinks?" Alexis called from the make-shift bar that had originally been a desk.

"All three of us," Alana called back, and Amanda began pouring some concoction.

Jessica was now a part of "us" in their minds. She settled back in the chair, the knots in her back loosening.

When Alexis brought their drinks, Destiny handed Jessica hers. "Be careful with your nails. They're still wet."

As Jessica sipped her rum and Coke—which would better be described as rum with a splash of soda on top—Destiny started on her right hand. "Thanks for letting us do this, Jessica. It's like going to sleepovers in high school again."

Jessica set her barely touched drink on the floor and laughed. "I should be the one thanking you guys for making me look presentable."

Destiny snorted. "You know you don't need any of this to look gorgeous. You're one of the lucky ones."

Jessica had nothing to say to that. Gorgeous? Acceptable, sure. Maybe pretty. Not gorgeous.

After an hour, the beautification kicked up a notch, from leisurely drink sipping and nail polishing into full-on transformation mode. Jessica felt as if she were on some makeover TV show.

Alana had put Jessica's hair up multiple ways before declaring, "Jessica, your hair is just too beautiful to hide. We have to keep it down," and undoing all her work.

While Alana fussed with her hair, adding more curl

here and there, Anna and Lindsey gave her smoky eyes, Amanda put dark lipstick on her full lips and who knew what else was added to her face.

Finally they had her squeeze into a black dress so low-cut that she knew exactly what would happen if she moved too quickly at any point during the evening, and God help her if she fell. It certainly would offer little resistance if she was doing any bouncing around at all. At least it was a full two inches longer than the one the previous night. She counted her blessings there.

A few minutes before eight, the women declared themselves finished. "You look fantastic!" Cindy said, and Jessica thought her friend might cry with happiness.

The other ladies nodded in agreement.

Jessica looked in the full-length mirror and studied her reflection, impressed with what she saw. Shocked, really.

This wasn't the regular Jessica she normally saw in the mirror at home. This was a super version of Jessica: Jessica 2.0. She was tall and beautiful and *sexy.* That had never been a word to describe her, but it certainly described this new version staring back at her.

She took a calming breath and turned away from the mirror, feeling a mix of discomfort and pride with the image she was projecting to the world.

As she followed the others out the door, she felt a small sense of foreboding. These shoes were even higher than the ones the night before, and with how low the scoop of the dress went—and the fact that she wasn't able to wear a bra with it—she was very aware what a dangerous combination it could be. It might end very badly indeed, if she wasn't careful.

Except for that little episode at the airport, she tended to be pretty steady on her feet, but the red heels she was wearing were something else entirely. She wished she could switch into a more reasonable pair, but the others insisted she looked amazing, and her mirror self agreed. So stilettos it would be.

On the outside, she looked like a woman from a club scene in a movie, the confident and attractive girl who would go home with a stranger if the mood took her. On the inside, she was still the unsure introvert who was on the defensive against anyone who might try to get too close. But she *wanted* to be that outside version, if even for just a weekend.

The group of women, dressed to the nines and ready to devastate the city's men, went down to the lobby to meet Marilyn's Jeremiah and whatever friend he was bringing along. Marilyn wrapped her arm through Cindy's. "So, Cindy, there is a possibility that Jeremiah and I might break away and have our own little party, if you don't mind. You can totally say no, though."

Jessica knew Cindy well enough to see that she was less than thrilled about one of their party taking off with a stranger, but Jessica knew she'd never say anything to that effect. She just smiled at Marilyn and said, "Of course! Have fun. How often are you in Vegas?"

It wasn't in Cindy to be anything but supportive of her friends' decisions. It was one of the reasons Jessica had called Cindy first when she and Russ broke up, and why she was planning on telling her about the whole embarrassing Aaron fascination she'd been having and the entire strip-club story. When they were safely back home, of course, and it could just be a funny Vegas anecdote.

As they walked up the few steps toward the lobby, Jessica watched her feet carefully to avoid an embarrassing tumble. When she was at the top of the stairs and looked up, Marilyn was moving quickly toward a smiling man, and—

And Aaron. She couldn't believe it. His eyes were taking in each girl, but when they landed on her, he stopped short, his eyebrows rising in surprise. They stared at each other in shock. Aaron was the friend Jeremiah was bringing to dinner; Jeremiah was the guy who'd been calling Aaron back to the group when he was drunkenly hitting on her. It all made ridiculous improbable sense.

The rest of the girls walked up to meet the men, but Jessica was frozen to the spot by his stare. Her cheeks flushed, her heart sped up so much she could feel it pressing against her chest.

You can do this. Just breathe and smile and walk forward, pretend this is normal.

Her silent pep talk did nothing to move her feet or stop her heart from slamming away. It didn't erase the look of astonishment and slight panic she knew was plastered across her face.

She didn't know if she wanted to run into his arms or back up to the hotel room, but neither of those involved casually walking up and shaking hands.

By this time, the other girls had met Jeremiah and

were being introduced to Aaron, who had to be smacked on the arm by Jeremiah in order to pull his attention away from her. She felt oddly pleased about the stunned expression on his face, and the way his eyes stayed on her until he was forced to acknowledge the others. Even Miss New York couldn't take away his focus from her.

Once Aaron's eyes finally shifted away, Jessica felt free—for the moment at least—to think and walk, but she couldn't stop her gaze from sliding down his well-cut suit jacket, to the fitted shirt underneath, to his dark blue jeans.

Everything looked as if it was made perfectly for his body, showing him off without looking intentional. Did he do that on purpose, or was that just how clothes looked on a body that magnificent?

She walked toward the men slowly and *very* carefully—she definitely didn't want to trip over her own feet now—but stayed behind the rest of the women so she wouldn't have to do something as mundane as shake his hand. There would be no way to keep from melting if she got too close to him.

Jessica tried to come up with a plan. She was usually great at having plans in difficult situations, but this time she was completely at sea with nothing to grab on to. She thought about her anger the night before, and about her thoughts when she'd seen him running. Oh, the running.

She was physically attracted to him, no doubt about that. More than she'd ever been to anyone. He clearly wasn't looking for anything serious this weekend, so why should she? She was a single woman in Vegas for a few days for a bachelorette party—didn't that give her the freedom to do anything without regret?

By the time they'd all started walking to dinner, she had begun telling herself that one night with the man of her dreams would be enough, that it was probably just a physical attraction she'd get over after acting upon it. She should go up and talk to him, at least. Smooth things out from when they'd last seen each other.

What she did, however, was stay as far away from him as possible and blush a fiery shade of scarlet that deepened every time he glanced her way, which he did every few seconds while they walked to the restaurant.

At dinner, she tried to place as many people between them as possible, but after she sat down, he slid into the chair next to her. Jessica cursed inwardly, feeling his stare as she looked everywhere possible but into his eyes. Sitting just a few inches from him, she could feel the heat coming off his body, and every inch of her skin felt as if it was being shot through with electrical currents. Her heart was beating so wildly, she was sure he could hear it, and the struggle to keep her breathing normal was pointless.

"Jessica," he half whispered, trying to get her attention.

When he said her name, his voice wrapped around her like a silky blanket, and she wanted, more than anything, for him to say it again. He didn't seem to realize that all of her attention was on him at the moment, no matter where she forced her eyes. She finally looked at him, her breath catching in her throat.

"Jessica," he whispered, and she felt that thrill again.

"I'm so sorry about my behavior last night. I was drunk and I was excited to see you again. I can't believe I did any of the things I did. I swear I'm not a drunken idiot. Most of the time."

His eyes were pleading for a positive response from her, a crooked sheepdog smile playing on his lips. He looked almost innocent and like someone who was just trying to make amends, but she could tell by the lower pitch of his voice, the darkness of his eyes and the tense hold of his sculpted jaw that he wasn't saying everything on his mind.

With mild astonishment, she understood what was happening. He was barely holding himself together, too. She had assumed that he thought she was attractive, but that he couldn't possibly be feeling the same thrill of sensations. But really, he wanted her as much as she wanted him.

An amazingly handsome cowboy wanted her with an intensity that cut down her already shaky control even more. Even if he just wanted this makeup-covered, cleavage-showing Jessica 2.0, that intensity was a surprise she hadn't expected.

She suddenly realized he was waiting for her to say something, but what could she say? She'd given herself permission to allow the physical attraction, but now that he was so close, so obviously wanting her, she wanted more than ever to run away and hide.

Jessica cleared her throat a little, giving her mind a chance to settle down. It didn't work. "It's fine. I'm sorry I got so upset at you over nothing, really. It was just a weird moment. Friends?" she asked.

No! her mind screamed at her. *Friends! Are you kidding? Not friends!* She wished she could drop under the table as soon as the words left her mouth. The last thing on earth she wanted at that moment was to just be friends. How could they be friends when they were only going to see each other for this one weekend, and spending even a few seconds near him made her want to jump out of her clothes and curl herself around his body?

She could see from the flexing muscles in his jaw that it hadn't been the word he'd wanted to hear, either, but he smiled at her, showing a row of perfect teeth she could almost imagine nibbling on her ear. "Okay. Friends. I'm Aaron."

Berating herself internally, she smiled back. "Hi, Aaron."

Although she'd memorized his name from the paper he'd given her, had looked at it so many times that she could picture the way he'd written every letter, that was the first time she'd said it out loud, and she felt a dropping sensation in her stomach as his eyes darkened a little more and his cheeks flushed, but not from embarrassment. She could feel the heat wafting off his body, could smell his intoxicating, indescribable manly scent and suddenly she felt far too close for comfort. She could hardly breathe.

It was too much for her to deal with at the moment. Shaky, she whispered quickly, "Would you excuse me?" and scooted herself away from the table.

In her hurry, her arm pressed against his, and the jolt of electricity made her move even faster. She rushed toward the bathroom, feeling his eyes still on her. The areas of her arm that had touched his sizzled with feeling, and some of the heat emanating off him seemed to have lodged itself firmly in her stomach.

She had loved Russ, but in a calm and comfortable way, like a good friend. Nothing she'd ever experienced had felt anything like this. This was something so new and terrifying that she didn't know what to make of it.

In the restroom was a small sitting area with a bench. She flopped herself down on it and dropped her head to her knees, breathing in deeply, trying to get control of herself. How was she going to get through the evening around Aaron? All she wanted to do was rip off his shirt and press herself against his bare chest, but she just couldn't do it. The only other alternative was to stay as far away from him as possible, but it didn't seem that he'd let that happen, based on how he magically ended up sitting next to her for dinner.

She spent a few minutes sitting there until her heart had slowed, then looked in the mirror and steeled herself for the evening, reminding her reflection to behave like an adult, like the cool sexy woman she appeared to be, and not allow some guy to get her so flustered.

Then she walked briskly out the door, turning sharply toward the dining area.

And walked smack into Aaron.

Jessica bounced off his chest and would have fallen to the floor, except that his arms curled around her to catch her. She regained her balance, but his arms stayed wrapped around her body. Her stilettos made her so tall that they were eye-to-eye. Everything she'd done to gain control immediately fell apart as she felt his arms wrapped around her, saving her. She could see the shock on his face, but his eyes only showed longing. For her.

"Whoa! I was just waiting to make sure you were okay. You'd been gone awhile and—"

His husky voice and arms around her made the last of her logic and fear crumble. Without thinking about what she was doing, she leaned forward and sealed her mouth to his, cutting off the spill of words. There was a moment of stillness as he realized what was happening, and then his hands slid up her back into her hair, leaving trails of sensation in their wake.

His right hand moved forward, cupping her jaw as he deepened the kiss, his tongue slipping inside her mouth, exploring her. Her arm wrapped around his neck and she pressed herself against his body. The eagerness with which he responded, the swelling she felt against her hip, only drove her desire over the edge, clouding her mind. If he hadn't been holding her so tightly, her legs would have given out beneath her.

Then the sound of a cell phone started, shrill and insistent, cutting through the moment.

They broke apart, and Aaron grumbled deep in his throat as he pulled the phone out of his pocket, one arm still wrapped around her. "Jeremiah," he muttered, and she couldn't help smiling at the tone of his voice, as if he would kill his friend if he got the chance.

She noticed that he was still holding her tight to his chest, but she couldn't find it in her to move away.

He answered, glaring daggers at the device, "Jeremiah? Yeah, do whatever you want. I'll message you later if I want to meet up, but if you don't hear from me, don't call."

She could hear Jeremiah laughing on the other end of the phone, and flushed, embarrassed, as she realized what Aaron had implied. Was she going to be another conquest by this rugged man who clearly had several notches in his belt?

Was that a bad thing? All she knew was that being so close to him, breathing him in, electrified her. Her mind was still fuzzy from the kiss.

He shoved the phone back into his pocket and looked at her, their faces just inches from each other. Neither had let go of the other. "Jeremiah and Marilyn are taking off. I don't know what his excuse was, something about walking around the art collection or something. They'll catch up with your friends later. Nobody's ordered food yet, but they decided they weren't hungry or something. What about you?"

The question hung between them, asking about so much more than food. She couldn't eat now if her life depended on it, but she couldn't just leave, could she? She was intoxicated with this man holding her so close, and there was nothing to hold her back if this was what she wanted. After a short pause, she decided to be impulsive for once.

"I'm not hungry. I'll text Cindy and let her know I'm going up to my room. She won't mind."

She turned her attention to her handbag, grabbing her phone and quickly sending a garbled text to that effect. She could feel him staring at her the entire time, and hardly knew what she was writing, so long as it was quick and meant she could disappear with this man. When she had finished, she looked back into his eyes, her breath catching in her throat.

She wanted to taste his lips again but had gotten enough of her mind back to realize that making out in the restroom hallway of a busy restaurant was probably not the best idea. To punctuate that thought, a woman skirted uncomfortably around them, heading toward the bathroom.

Jessica finally pulled away from him, realizing as she did so that her top had gone askew during their embrace, leaving one of her breasts exposed. She flushed and fixed herself hurriedly, suddenly feeling her modesty and embarrassment return now that she wasn't quite so close to him.

She looked up at his face. Aaron's eyes were staring directly at her cleavage. He had definitely noticed the clothing mishap. She flushed an even deeper red and almost changed her mind about the whole thing, but then he spoke, his voice had an even deeper huskiness than before. "You're staying at this hotel, right?"

It sent thrills through her, and she could only answer with a "Yes."

She waited, unsure of herself. Kissing him had made her blood rise and the bottom drop out of her stomach. It was something she'd never felt before and longed to feel again, but she wasn't sure how to recreate the moment.

He seemed to sense her uncertainty. "Should we—"

He paused, clearly waiting for her to fill in the gap, to make a decision. She looked at his eyes again and threw caution and inhibition out the window. "Let's go," she said softly, stepping in to brush her lips against his once more, to remind herself why she was making this decision, more than anything else.

Her mouth paused against his for just a moment as his tongue flicked lightly against hers, and then she grabbed his hand and, on shaky legs, began leading him away from the restaurant. If she didn't get somewhere private quickly, she wasn't sure she'd be able to control herself any longer. His fingers threaded with hers, and each point of contact felt alive with intensity. She wanted to feel that all over her body, and didn't want to resist that urge for any longer than she needed to.

Even if it was just one night, she had to have him. Had to feel what it would be like to sleep with this man she barely knew, but who her body reached out for with such desperation, the way a person lost in the desert would reach for a glass of water. Her mind was still arguing against it, telling her that it wasn't a logical choice, but the voice in her head had gotten so faint and overwhelmed by her firing nerves that it was barely heard, easily dismissed.

Somehow she made it to the elevator with him in tow without falling or wrapping herself around him in the middle of the casino floor. As soon as the doors slid shut and the elevator began its ascent to her floor, they flung themselves at each other again.

As she kissed him, deeply and hungrily, his hand found its way along her stomach, then slid around to the small of her back, the friction of his hand against the material of her dress increasing her body's tension. Her skin was so sensitive that every movement caused trem-

ors of excitement to flow through her. She could feel
that his body was rock hard against her, and his pants
were barely up to the challenge of holding him back.

The elevator dinged and the doors slid open, but as
she began to pull away to exit, the arm wrapped around
her waist tightened and held her against him, her feet
hovering above the floor, his lips still on her. He had
lifted her enough so he could kiss along her jawline and
her neck, and stepped off the elevator with her in his
arms, making her feel as though tiny explosions were
going off in her brain.

"What room?" he growled into her neck, letting loose
waves of electricity in the spots warmed by his breath.

A tingle went down her spine as she heard the complete abandon in his voice. He wasn't in control of himself, and she had the feeling it wasn't something that
happened to him very often. She liked it.

She looked around wildly for a second, desperate to
find her room. She finally realized which door it was
and pointed. He let her feet hit the floor, and she pulled
him along toward the door. As she turned toward the
door, grabbing randomly through her bag for the key
card, he stood behind her, pressing himself against her,
his hand rubbing against her stomach as his perfect
teeth nibbled on one ear.

After what felt like ages, she found the card and
managed to slide it home. Finally they were in the room
together and the door closed behind them. Before she
had even a second to think, she was pressed against the
door, his lips once again on hers. The kiss was long and
deep, and the feel of his tongue plundering her mouth,

then his teeth biting lightly at her bottom lip, silenced any last appeals from her voice of reason.

Suddenly he pulled back from her and looked into her eyes in the dark room only lit by the glitz of the city through the window. "Are you sure?" he asked.

At first she was confused. Didn't he realize how much she wanted him? Then she remembered that within twenty-four hours she had stormed away from him, tried to ignore him and told him she wanted to be friends. Not exactly the clearest signals.

She closed the gap he had created between them, and decided that honesty would be best here. "I'm sure, Aaron—"

She didn't need to worry about explaining any more than that, because the moment she gave the green light, he pressed his mouth to hers again and his hands began exploring her body, as if he needed to feel every inch of her skin. As he stroked the skin where the top of her dress exposed her cleavage, she gasped at the intensity of the feeling. Her nipples were taut and sensitive, yearning for his touch, and the slight brush of his hand only made it worse. Her hand quickly went to the back of the dress and dragged down the zipper without her thinking about it, allowing the dress to fall, leaving her in nothing more than her rather plain black underwear.

Since the ending of her previous relationship, she'd gotten rid of most of her sexy underthings, but she was glad she was at least wearing black to match the dress. Being sensual wasn't natural for her, and she felt a little embarrassed. Was she supposed to make some kind of move? Did she even *have* moves?

Her mental litany of self-consciousness ended abruptly, though, as he looked her up and down, breathed a quick "Wow" and grabbed her close once more, his head dipping down to her neck as his fingers continued to explore. She started fumbling with the buttons on his shirt.

This lack of control was so different it was hard to wrap her mind around it. All she knew was that she wanted him naked, wanted to be pressed against his body. The heat radiating from his skin made her feel deliciously warm, and she wanted it all.

He shrugged out of his shirt, and it was her turn to be amazed. His stomach and chest were even more impressive than she had imagined. His masculinity emanated off him in waves of heat and strength and longing. Her hands ran over his chest, his stomach and up along the rippling muscles of his arms.

In one quick movement, he gathered her up in his arms, and she laughed breathlessly from surprise and delight as her feet left the floor. He carried her over toward the bed, still running his tongue and teeth along her neck until he hit a sweet spot in the hollow of her neck. She moaned from the feeling, and whispered his name, and he sucked deeper, intensifying the experience. She felt her body quickening. It had been so long since any man kissed her, and never like this.

Then his mouth found her nipple and began teasing it greedily as his fingers moved lower and lower until a single finger dipped into her folds, and she gasped, her back arching as the tension built low in her belly. Any moment she would fly over the cliff.

His fingers danced on her every nerve as his teeth

scraped against her skin, sending her over the edge. She cried out, her back curving even more with the strength of her orgasm. As the waves washed over her, she could see him leaning over her, watching her body react.

As the tremors subsided, he smiled and tucked her hair behind her ear. "I've barely gotten started," he whispered into her ear, sending fresh waves of pleasure through her.

She pulled his mouth back to hers and kissed him again, one hand moving to his waist. She wasn't done with him yet. As her fingers moved across the bare skin of his abs, Aaron groaned with pleasure, and it made her feel sexier than she'd ever felt.

Jessica unhooked his belt and unbuttoned his jeans, allowing her hand to brush against his hardness through the rough denim. He laughed deep in his throat, and, his voice barely a whisper, he said, "You are way too sexy."

It was her turn to smile, feeling more powerful than ever. She leaned over and moved her mouth to his jaw, kissing the rough jawline as she worked her way down to his chest.

5

AARON COULDN'T BELIEVE what was happening. Since he'd seen Jessica walking toward him with the group of girls that Jeremiah had made plans with, he'd been in a blur of unreality.

He had been so sure he had lost the chance to kiss those amazing lips, to touch that achingly beautiful skin.

And now they were in her room and every inch of his body was alive, feeling her soft, supple body up against him, running his fingers through her hair, tingling with sensation as she ran her hands along his chest, her tongue following after. When she had begun undoing his pants, he thought he would burst under her fingers.

She was kissing down along his chest with an agonizing slowness that knocked the wind out of him. He could see her body shaking, still taut and sensitive from her climax. He rubbed his fingers lightly down her back, making her shiver again.

Touching her and watching her react had been surreal, and had made him want her even more, if that was possible. He sat up, lifting her face toward him with a hand curved gently under her jaw, and he kissed her again, letting the feel of it run down through his body. He slipped her panties slowly down her long, elegant legs and looked up at her, questioning, one last time. She smiled at him, her lips thick and dark, her eyes showing her longing for him. He let the last of his clothing fall to the floor, tore open the wrapper of a condom and sheathed himself, then moved toward where she lay on the bed.

She leaned forward, kissing him as he moved closer to her. Then he was above her, pressing her into the soft pillows, one leg between hers. She moved her thighs apart slowly, as if reluctant, and he leaned back, looking into her eyes, afraid this wasn't what she wanted.

"Is this okay?" he asked, praying she wouldn't stop this.

She looked very serious for a moment, as if she was thinking through the situation. That didn't bode well. She said, "Just this one weekend, and then we never see each other again, right?"

He didn't know exactly what answer she wanted, but he gave her the truth. He nodded.

She put her hand on the nape of his neck, pulled him back toward her and opened for him. She looked him deep in the eye and wrapped her legs around him. The only thing she said was his name, just a quick, half whispered "Aaron."

When she said his name in that breathy, intense way, everything melted away but their two bodies. He slid into her, and was jolted with the perfection of the moment. He watched her face contort as they moved together, and the world seemed very far away and unimportant. The only thing that mattered was this moment caught in time, this beautiful woman, these electrifying sensations.

He refused to think about the next day, let alone home and the years ahead. Instead he focused on the night that lay ahead of them. He had all night to make love to Jessica, and he was going to make sure they both enjoyed it fully.

They rocked with each other slowly, then faster and faster until he couldn't take it anymore, and he teased and touched and dragged her over with him.

"Wow," was all she said after catching her breath.

He had to agree. Everything about her was spectacular.

He wrapped his arms around her, enjoying the feel of her body against his. "You smell good," she murmured sleepily into his chest.

He chuckled. "Thanks. So do you. And your skin is so soft."

She didn't reply, and he looked down to see that she was already dozing off. He pulled her in a little closer and slept, too.

NEAR MORNING, JUST as the sky was lightening to a soft gray, Aaron stared at her, the mysterious airport woman, who was sleeping peacefully on his chest, his arm wrapped around her, his hand resting on her hip. She was more than beautiful; she was miraculous.

When he woke again, it was full morning and he was alone in the bed. He looked around and spied Jessica sitting in the chair at the desk wearing a robe, typing away on her computer. He could see her face staring intently at the screen in the mirror on the wall in front of her. She was without makeup, tousled and beautiful. He wanted to walk up behind her and put his hands on her again, just to feel her warmth and her skin against his.

For a second, though, he wasn't sure what he should do. Would she feel differently about their night together in the light of day? What if she asked him to leave?

He didn't know what would happen, but he knew he wanted to spend more time around this woman who made him feel alive. His mysterious airport girl, his unlikely fantasy, had become more than he would've imagined, and he didn't want to let that go until he had to.

She stopped typing and looked up into the mirror at him, smiling a little awkwardly. He smiled back. Maybe she wasn't too sure about things, either. The silence hung between them. Finally, just to break the slight tension, he said the only thing his racing brain could settle on.

"Hey."

Her smile softened. "Hi."

"Listen, Jessica, I—"

She stopped him with a wave of her hand. "No, it's fine. You don't have to say anything. I understand. Feel free to go whenever you like."

Her coolness stabbed, and he wasn't sure what to do except be honest. "I was going to say that last night was incredible, and I was wondering if you'd want to spend the day with me. But if you don't that's fine. I can just go," he ended in a rush.

She jumped up. "Oh! No, that would be good! I just… I just didn't want to make you feel obligated or anything, and I wasn't sure…" Her voice trailed off.

His smile returned, and his heart warmed at her flustered explanation. He tried not to notice that her robe had fallen open slightly as she turned toward him, but the sliver of flesh was distracting and his body responded. "Great. What do you want to do?"

She looked at the bed; then her eyes roved over his body, only partially covered by a sheet, and he smiled wider, realizing where her mind had gone. His body flooded with heat, and he leaned up a little more to hide his arousal.

She apparently managed to gain control of her thoughts, because she looked him in the eye and, a touch too casually, said, "Anything. I just got some work done and Cindy doesn't expect to see me until later this afternoon. I think they had a really late night, so I probably won't even hear from her for hours."

"What kind of work?" he asked.

Part of him wanted to avoid discussing the real world, not find out anything about her job, her family, her life. It was too dangerous, if she was as interesting as he suspected. But another part of him just wanted to hear her talk some more.

When she spoke, her voice was halting. "I'm an editor. But I don't think we should talk about—I mean, I think this should—"

She broke off, but he got what she was saying loud

and clear. "No details. Sure. 'What happens in Vegas stays in Vegas' kind of a thing."

She narrowed her eyes for a moment and he was worried she was going to ask him exactly how many times he'd done something similar. It would be impossible to explain how this was different, and he couldn't see any way *that* conversation would end well.

Luckily the expression faded and she just nodded. "Vegas only. That sounds perfect."

"Okay, no details. Just a fun weekend. How about we go downtown? I haven't been there in forever, and that's about as Vegas as you can get."

She glanced again at the bed, and her face showed disappointment for a half second, but then her smile returned. "Sure. I'll need to shower, but I could be ready to go in twenty minutes."

He stood up and walked toward her, allowing her eyes to roam over his naked, aroused body. Nearly losing his cool demeanor because of the intense scrutiny, he picked her up out of the chair. "Oh, I think we'll need longer than that."

She laughed as he nuzzled open her robe a little more and set her down on the bed, and the sound was so happy that he couldn't wait to hear it again.

"What did you have in mind?" she asked, the laughter still in her voice.

"Oh, I'm sure we can come up with a few things," he answered.

They kissed, long and deep, without the rush and desperation of the night before. Jessica slid one leg around him, her body exposed to him as he leaned over her. When they finally came up for air, she slowly slid her leg back across him until her thighs were closed and said, "Just what kind of woman do you think I am?" as she half-attempted to close her robe. Her grin was wicked and teasing.

Aaron's hand managed to catch one of her breasts before the robe closed completely, stroking it until her smile turned genuine and she leaned back to give him more access, letting the robe fall back open.

"I think you're an incredibly sexy woman who plans on having a very fun weekend torturing me," he answered.

She laughed again and her leg slid back around him. As his mouth closed on hers once more, his hand slipped lower, down the fluttering muscles of her stomach until he reached her folds, making her gasp.

He waited until she was squirming and almost begging him to don the condom and move on top of her.

In the morning, it was slow and almost painfully wonderful as he slid inside her again. Her back arched and he watched as she closed her eyes, her mouth formed into a perfect circle. This was going to be the best weekend of his life.

And quite possibly the hardest to get over.

When they were both spent, he rolled to the side and watched her face relax as the intensity of her climax dissipated. A smile played on the edges of her lips.

Finally, after they caught their breath, she stood. He took in her entire, lithe body. She grabbed her robe as though she was going to put it on, then hesitated and set it back down. He was glad she'd decided not to cover herself—he loved looking at her.

She pointed to the bathroom and said, "I need to take a shower."

He didn't want to assume he was invited, so he waited a moment, listening to the blood shoot through his veins. It felt more like fire. He raised his eyebrows in question.

"You want to join me?"

Aaron didn't need to be asked twice. He was out of the bed and next to her in a flash, his hand on the small of her back. She laughed her loud, ringing laugh. "So that's a yes?"

She had the best laugh.

The warm water was soothing, and he was again intrigued by this girl, with her interesting mix of shyness and provocative power. He couldn't say if she was self-confident or self-conscious or both. He just couldn't peg her into any one hole.

He shampooed her hair and soaped her body, massaging every inch of skin he could touch, just as he had fantasized only the day before. The shower took much longer than either of them would have expected, but he certainly wasn't going to complain.

They dried and dressed, and Jessica called room service and ordered a large breakfast since they hadn't eaten the night before. As they ate and talked, Aaron immediately realized that Jessica was *smart*. He'd dated a few smart girls, but none of them were quick and clever like her, and he reveled in the knowledge.

"So, were you going to call me?" he asked after a

brief pause in the conversation. It was a dangerous question, but he needed to know the answer.

She pressed her lips together for only a moment, but it was enough to see that she didn't like the question. "I was considering it, but I lost your number."

"Lost it?" How could she have lost it?

"Well, I didn't lose it, exactly. I tossed it in the trash after..."

"After I was an asshole at a strip club." Why did she have to see him at his absolute worst like that? "I'm sorry, again, about that. Not my finest moment."

She shrugged, as if it didn't matter. He wanted to tell her that it *did* matter, that he wasn't that guy, but the words died in his throat. The worst thing was that in some ways her image of him was true.

It wasn't a happy thought. He pushed it aside. "Well, it looks like I lost a perfectly good bookmark. Serves me right, I guess."

She seemed to pick up on the need to change the topic, because she didn't even flinch at the abrupt shift. "What were you reading? Something rodeo-themed? Like *The History of Cowboy Hats* or something?"

Aaron paused. He should have expected that question, but he didn't want to tell her and have her think he was stupid. What a terrible change of topic "I'd rather not say" was.

Jessica shifted so her legs were tucked underneath her in the chair, and she leaned over the empty plates toward him, her eyes wide with interest. "Come on! You have to tell me. It's more embarrassing than *The*

History of Cowboy Hats? Was it *Fifty Shades*? It was, wasn't it?"

He couldn't help smiling at her excitement. It didn't look as though she was going to give up. "I'm reading *Harry Potter*," he confessed.

She leaned forward even more, giving him a pleasant view of her cleavage. "Ooh. Which one? Are you one of those *Harry Potter* fans who reads all of them over and over?"

"No, this is my first time reading the series. I'm on *The Goblet of Fire*. They're good, but I'm not some crazy fan or anything."

A sudden shift in her eyes made him smile. "How many times have you read them? Be honest," he wheedled.

She looked so cute when she was embarrassed. "I'm going to plead the Fifth," she finally answered.

Aaron considered pushing for the real answer, but he decided to let it be. It was enough to know that she didn't think he was weird for enjoying a bunch of kids' books. Jeremiah had given him so much crap for reading them that it was a nice change of pace to be around someone who clearly thought they were as much fun as he did.

They moved on to discuss movies and favorite shows, and the more they talked, the more he found he liked her. How could he not like a girl who loved *Die Hard*? If it wasn't for her love of *Sex and the City* reruns, he would have wondered if Jeremiah or someone had paid a woman to pretend she was the perfect match for him.

"*Sex and the City* is a great show. You're not allowed to hate it if you haven't seen it," she insisted.

"I'll take your word for it. I'm not going to watch it," he answered, loving how her forehead wrinkled when she had that earnest look on her face.

He noticed they were both very careful to steer clear of anything personal. He wanted to ask what kind of editing she did, exactly, but stopped himself. Part of him didn't even want to know what city she was from. He felt as if bringing up their real lives would remind them of the expiration date looming so close on their weekend. He was also slightly worried that she wasn't completely unattached, which would explain some of her reluctant behavior, and he didn't want to find out if that was the case and end this whole thing.

She seemed content to just enjoy their time together, and he didn't want to ruin that by discussing anything outside the present.

As they walked down to the elevator, he laced his fingers through hers, happy to be able to at least pretend she was his. They strolled through the lobby and got into the car he had ordered for them, not letting go. The grin she gave him as she slid into her seat was such a genuinely happy smile that lit up her eyes, and it settled into a warm spot deep in his chest.

When they arrived downtown, they wandered through the classic casinos, looking at the fish tanks and the golden nuggets that were displayed for the tourists, and meandered along Fremont Street. He nodded toward one of the casinos and said, "Do you want to do any gambling or anything? I don't want you to miss out on any of the Vegas stuff you planned on doing because I'm around."

Jessica tilted her head a little as she looked around. "Well, I just came in for the bachelorette party, so my plan was to hide in my room whenever I got the chance. Now that I'm out, we could do something like that. I don't know how to play any of the games, though."

"Do you know how to play blackjack?" She shook her head. "Want to learn?" he asked.

She scrunched her face, as if the topic was a little bit of a sore one for her. "I don't really have much extra money to give to the casinos, but we could play a little bit."

"You don't have to use your money. We can play with mine."

The look she gave him made it abundantly clear what she thought of that. He stopped her before she could argue. "Don't say no yet. Just think of it this way—I'd like to play, and I want to teach you how. It would be fun for me."

She still looked uncertain, so he gave her his biggest "now I'm begging" look, and her expression softened. Reluctantly, she answered, "Fine, but we're not spending ridiculous amounts of money at this. I don't need that kind of stress."

He wondered why she was so tight on money but didn't ask. Staying away from details was becoming hard already, and it was far less fun than it had seemed at first. He wanted to know more things about her.

They sat down at the cheapest table they could find and he bought in. When he tried to put three hundred-dollar bills on the table, Jessica pulled two of them back and shook her head, as if he'd just done something completely insane. He put the two bills away and scooted his chair close to hers under the guise of helping her. With his leg pressing against hers, it didn't matter how much money was on the table.

Though she'd never played before, he was impressed to see how quickly she picked up the game's logic and how confident she was in her ability to make the right choice. After only a few hands, she was hitting and staying as though she had played for years.

Most women he'd sat at a table with at various rodeo weekends would constantly ask what to do or make plays that didn't make sense. They'd giggle and shrug when they lost.

Jessica was not like most women. She watched the cards with such intensity Aaron was half worried one of the pit bosses would think she was counting cards, except for the fact that she refused to play more than the minimum five dollars a hand and panicked a little every time she needed to double her bet. Watching her amused him no end. She was cute when she was anxious.

When the dealer placed an ace on the queen in front of Jessica, she gave Aaron a brilliant smile and clapped her hands a little. "I got blackjack! What do I get, seven dollars? What am I going to buy with all that?"

He gave her his most confused look. "Why do you think you get the seven dollars? We're playing with my money, remember?"

She rolled her eyes and shoved her shoulder against his, grumbling. He laughed and held up his hands to make it clear he was joking. Sitting next to her was worth it, even if she lost every penny of his money.

The dealer, a man about Aaron's age whose name tag identified him as Cody, smiled at them. "You two seem to be having a nice time. Are you just in town for the weekend?"

Aaron and Jessica exchanged a split-second glance. They both realized what he thought, but it didn't seem worth explaining the situation to this stranger. He wasn't sure what he would say, anyway. They both nodded.

Aaron could tell Cody was going to ask him some more questions and headed him off. "How long have you lived in Vegas, Cody?"

Cody said, "Oh, about six years now. It's not a bad place, once you get used to it."

Jessica studied her cards thoughtfully, and Aaron could practically hear the gears whirring in her head as she tried to remember what to do in that situation. She stayed—the right move, of course—and looked back to the dealer. "What made you move out here?"

Cody flipped his card, took another and busted. As he paid them, he said, "I came out here for school. It's much cheaper to live here than it was in California. I'm finishing up a law degree at the university."

Before he could say more, another dealer came up and tapped him on the shoulder. Cody said, "It was nice to meet you. Enjoy the rest of your weekend. It's always great to see two people in love."

He left before Aaron could respond. Not that he had anything to say to that. He almost didn't want to look at Jessica and see her reaction. What if she agreed with

Cody? What if she scoffed at the idea? Neither sounded particularly appealing.

Jessica's hand dropped to his thigh and squeezed his leg, sending a thrill up through his groin and settling in his stomach. She knocked him with her shoulder again. "You hear that, sweetie? We must be quite adorable."

Aaron couldn't quite bring himself to joke about it, but he smiled at her. The silence lingered for a minute. He didn't think he'd be able to stand it much longer. Luckily Jessica looked down at her chips. "Well, I think I understand the game, and it looks like we made you twenty bucks. Shall we go?"

Aaron agreed, glad to change the topic. They took their chips to the cashier. Aaron had lost a little of his fifty, but Jessica was up over thirty. When he tried to hand it to her, she pushed it back at him. "There is no way I'm keeping that," she said.

He looked at the money and considered the options. "How about we use it for food or something?"

"That works for me. I'm a *huge* fan of food."

She was being deliberately casual, trying to get past the whole "in love" thing. Aaron wasn't sure if he was grateful or irritated about it. There was no point lingering on it, though. Their weekend would be over soon enough, and there wasn't time to waste on wondering about a passing remark from a dealer.

Jessica thankfully broke the silence before it could get too thick around them. "How do you play the other games?"

Something to talk about. Perfect. He rattled off descriptions of pai gow, craps and casino war—which was easy, since she knew war, and it was pretty much that with betting—and he could practically see her absorbing the information and filing it away in her brain. It was a wonderful thing to watch.

He wondered what it would be like to sit across from her at a poker table; he imagined she'd quickly become a force to be reckoned with. He doubted they would have time for it this weekend, but maybe next time—

He cut off the thought. Someone else would need to teach her that.

He examined her, focusing on her beautiful eyes and the strands of hair falling against her cheek. He imagined her glancing at her cards, her manner cool and confident whatever they might be, and tossing her chips all in with that little smile he'd seen play across her face throughout their night together. The mental image shifted seamlessly to one of her sitting on the poker table and wrapping her legs around him, unbuttoning his shirt—and he had to stop it there when he remembered they were in public.

He breathed deeply, keeping his body from getting aroused through sheer force of will. Aaron wanted her again. He loved feeling every part of her, the explosive reactions as he buried himself in her, saw her eyes close and heard her breath catch with pleasure. He wanted them to get out from the cloud that was hovering over them, get back to where they had been that morning. What better way was there than licking the small spot at the base of her neck that made her tremble?

He couldn't spend too much time considering that, or he'd be grabbing her and running back for the car. He didn't want her to think he was some oversexed cave-man, and based on that encounter at the strip club, that could very well be her impression of him even now. He hoped she saw he was more than that.

"Did you want to try any of them out?" he asked after he finished explaining the games.

Jessica shook her head. "I think I better quit while I'm ahead. I don't want to lose all of my winnings, and it looks like luck isn't on your side today. You might end up being one of those guys flying home without his shirt because he lost it at the tables in Sin City."

Aaron was pretty sure luck was very much on his side this weekend, if the woman with him was any in-dication. And if he ended up flying home without his shirt, it would have something to do with her, as well.

He was getting too attached to this woman who would disappear out of his life in two days, or even earlier. He had no idea when her flight home was. The most rational part of his mind told him to break it off before he got invested any deeper into the relationship, but he knew he wouldn't do that.

"Let's get some fresh air, then," he said, nodding toward the door.

As she moved to the exit, he stood a little behind her, watching her gorgeous form as she strode through the banks of slot machines. How anybody could keep their attention on those things as she walked by was a mystery.

Although he definitely wasn't in love as Cody as-sumed, he couldn't give up an incredible weekend with this mind-blowing woman, even if it meant it would hurt to leave and never see her again. It would only hurt a little, he promised himself.

He just needed to soak up everything he could get until their time in Vegas was up.

6

As they walked down Fremont Street, Jessica studied Aaron, wondering what was running through his mind. It was probably something about what that damn dealer said. He could be freaking out, thinking she wanted a relationship and just call the rest of the weekend off.

God, she hoped that didn't happen. When she'd first seen him, her thoughts were so focused on the sexual charge running through her and the images of his body against hers that she didn't take the time to think about his personality. But after they'd spent the morning together talking and exploring, she found that she was enjoying his company more and more. His mind was sharp, and she couldn't always tell what he was thinking—she liked that. And now she might lose out on another two days of it?

No way she was going to let that happen. She needed to think of some way to get them past the awkward moment. But her mind blanked.

"You should learn how to play Texas Hold'em. You'd be good at it," he said, breaking her reverie.

She smiled. Exactly the kind of diversion she'd been searching for. "Actually I know how to play that."

He gave her a sidelong glance. "You know poker, but not blackjack? That's a weird combination."

"I do some editing for a writer friend of mine, and he wrote a book where the characters played poker. So I learned how to play to make sure it was all accurate. They never played blackjack."

He laughed. "Have you actually played poker? Like, with real people?"

"Well, no, but I watched some videos of the pros. I understand the game. I'm probably better at it than you are."

It was a bald-faced lie—she had no doubt she was terrible—but needling him would be fun, and maybe it would bring back that little half smile he did sometimes.

Sure enough, it appeared when he raised his eyebrows at her. "Seriously, Jessica? I'm from Texas. I've played Texas Hold'em my whole life. I'd destroy you."

Even though she knew she'd lose, the challenge was too much to resist. "Sometime this weekend, we'll grab a pack of cards and play."

She wasn't sure what she liked more: the dare in his eyes or the fact that she now knew where he was from. She had figured a lot of the cowboys in town for the rodeo weren't *actually* cowboys. But Aaron was from Texas, cowboy central.

She pictured him standing in the middle of a barn, shirt off, leather-gloved hands pulling large bales of hay out for animals while the song from the truck commercials played in the background. The rugged mental image sent another thrill through her, in spite of how ridiculous it was.

She tried to shrug it off. She would never know if that image was at all accurate, because she refused to brook the subject of details from their outside life any more than they already had. Vegas only. Besides the offhanded comment, he seemed in no hurry to do so, either. He didn't actually say he lived on a ranch, either, just that he was from Texas. He could be an accountant there, for all she knew.

It was definitely for the best for a weekend fling. It might've even been better, safer, if they didn't know each other's names, but she did love the way his eyes flashed when she said his, and the warm feeling that rushed through her when he said hers, especially when he said it in that deep whisper as they were pressed together.

"You're on, Jessica," he said, smirking.

He was talking about poker, she knew, but in her mind the topic had become very different, indeed.

She tried to stop the flow of thoughts, reminding herself that they were still outside, around people, and she couldn't expect him to be ready to jump back into bed so soon. With Russ, twice in as many days had been a big deal, and despite how incredible their night—and morning—had been, she couldn't expect Aaron to just hop to attention because she wanted more.

She didn't know how she could still be so fired up, either. Sex had never before been such an experience that she couldn't get enough of it, but here she was, just hours after a romp-filled night, and every touch of his hand sent sparks through her, her heart thumping wildly, and her body yearned for him as much as ever.

She shook her head, trying to focus on the beautiful clear sky, the fresh air, the strange sights of old Las Vegas. The conversation quieted and they walked side by side, content to be near each other, their fingers lightly twined.

When her phone beeped, she looked down at it, confused. Why would anyone want to interrupt her peace?

It was a text from Cindy asking if she felt okay and if she wanted to come over to hang out.

Jessica grimaced. God, she was such a jerk, spending her time with Aaron without explaining to her friend what was going on. And it wasn't something she could explain in a text message.

She turned to Aaron. "I need to make a quick call. I'll be back in a minute."

"Oh. Okay," he answered, shifting a little awkwardly.

It took her a moment before she figured out what was wrong. When she realized he was probably thinking she was calling a boyfriend or something, she added, "Cindy, the bachelorette, texted me and I need to call her."

His relief was obvious when he nodded, and she broke away, her hand lingering in his an extra second before she finally untangled her fingers and walked over to an area away from the main thoroughfare. So Aaron didn't like the idea of being "the other guy." That was a good sign.

Except it didn't matter much because in a few days she would never see him again. Why did she need to keep reminding herself of that?

She tapped on her friend's name and pressed the phone to her ear. As it connected, she covered her eyes with her free hand, completely unsure of what she was going to say when Cindy picked up.

"Hey, Jessica! How's it going? You feeling better?"

Jessica was glad Cindy couldn't see her blushing. "Cindy, look, I have to tell you something. I wasn't sick, and I know we're here for your bachelorette party—"

Cindy cut her off with loud laughter before she could go any further. "Did you really think I wouldn't figure out exactly what was going on? Like I don't know you're with that guy, Jeremiah's friend? Come on, give me some credit. You thought I didn't notice how you blushed when you looked at him? Or the way you both disappeared, and then I get a sudden text from you that was nearly incomprehensible? Or the fact that he never came back? How about when I saw you booking it across the restaurant leading him by the hand as he followed like an excited puppy? You don't need to be Sherlock to figure it out."

Jessica groaned, more embarrassed than ever. "I was that obvious? God, Cindy, I'm sorry. I feel like an idiot."

"It was so obvious, but it's okay. He's gorgeous. Seriously, if I wasn't getting married… Anyway, just as long as you're sure you aren't setting yourself up to get hurt."

Jessica could hear the caution in her friend's voice, and she smiled at the concern. "Don't worry, I'm very aware of what's going on. We're only here for two days, anyway. It's just…it's just fun."

"Good. Well, are you still with him? What are you up to? You don't need to tell me if it's not an appropriate conversation topic."

Jessica could hear the laughter in her friend's voice. "We're at Fremont Street, downtown. Just wandering around."

"Okay. Well, I won't bother you. I'm glad you're finally being irresponsible. The girls and I are going shopping later this afternoon, and you know what we've got planned tonight, so if you want to catch up with us, just text."

More bars and clubs were on the menu again. Jessica looked over at Aaron and guessed she wouldn't be making it to any of that. She said goodbye to Cindy and hung up, making her way back to where Aaron was standing, waiting and looking at ridiculously glitzy Vegas paraphernalia.

As she approached, he held up a touristy shirt with Las Vegas written across it in sparkles and glitter. "What do you think?" he asked her. "Is it me?"

She laughed and said, "No, but if you get it, I'll wear it for you in the hotel room. It'll *probably* be long enough to cover me."

She blushed slightly at her uncharacteristically brazen statement, and closed the gap between them, leaning her body against his. It was so much fun to be this version of herself around him that she couldn't help it.

He raised his eyebrows at her questioningly, but his eyes darkened as his imagination took hold. When he spoke, his voice was low. "It's a little short, and you're really tall. I'm not sure it would, but I would love to see you try, Jessica. And I have the thirty dollars you won. We need to spend it on something."

She could feel the beginnings of his arousal at her hip. Her desire roared fully to life, and she again wished they were someplace a little more private. She leaned in a little closer and kissed him softly on his jaw, rough with stubble. She paused, wanting to kiss him more fully but able to control herself enough to pull away. That moment had been more than enough to make the feeling on her hip much more insistent.

She stepped back a half step, allowing some space, as much to give herself a chance to regain control as for him. He let out a shuddering breath and seemed to be holding on to the shirt rack for support. Jessica looked in his eyes and saw that he was doing everything he could to stop himself from pulling her down onto the ground, and it made her skin prickle with desire.

She leaned in again, close to his ear, and whispered to him, "We don't need the shirt."

She had barely finished before he'd tossed it back on the rack and was gripping her hand tightly, practically running back toward the car. She followed behind, laughing at her own strange behavior, except it didn't seem funny at all. Just wonderful and exciting.

She normally would never say or do anything like that, even with a man she'd been sleeping with. But something about Aaron made her feel sexy, and his immediate reaction only added to her enjoyment. She would never have described herself as sexy until this weekend. Suddenly that was exactly what she was, and she loved how it felt.

The driver was waiting patiently in the car for them, so she and Aaron were hardly seated before they were off toward his hotel. As soon as they were in the relative privacy of the backseat, Aaron pulled Jessica in for a long, deep kiss. She could feel his hunger matching hers, and before long they were barely holding back from undressing each other. The confines of their seat belts and the vague notion that the driver was just a few feet away were the only things stopping them.

When they broke apart, they were both flushed, and Aaron's pants were bulging with his erection. Jessica wanted to reach for the button on his jeans, but she restrained herself, knowing he'd have to calm down a bit before they arrived at the hotel so they could make it to the elevators and his room without being arrested.

She leaned away from him, taking deep breaths to calm herself. He did the same, but his eyes stayed locked to hers, and she could feel the electricity building in the few feet of air between them. It was too much, to the point where she began to feel claustrophobic, so she looked out the window at his hotel just a few blocks away.

She hadn't been to his room yet, but he'd mentioned that it was at the Hard Rock. Based on the giant flashing guitar glittering at the entrance, she imagined it was very different from the swanky hotels that had begun to overrun the Strip.

By the time the driver pulled up to the entrance, her heart had slowed down enough for her to at least appear calm when getting out of the car, but Aaron came up next to her and wrapped his arm around her waist, causing it to speed up again. His fingers moved up and down slightly, touching her stomach and hip, and it created an aching sensation in her gut. She wanted those fingers all over her, and the knowledge that they would be in just a few minutes made her nearly lose her balance.

His strong arm around her, she let him guide her to the elevators. She was close enough to him that she could smell the sweat on his skin and feel the heat from his body. His labored breathing made it clear that he wasn't anywhere near being as cool and collected as he appeared to be. In fact, she was quite sure that a quick graze of her teeth against his earlobe would be enough to drop him to the floor in the middle of the casino.

She wasn't exactly fully in her right mind, either, she had to admit. She hardly registered the loud music and dark atmosphere that was more akin to a club than a hotel, and it was only when they'd gotten to the elevators that she realized she had no idea what the area she'd just walked through actually looked like. She'd been too focused on the man by her side, his arm curled around her back, his fingers dancing along her side.

She was hoping to continue from where they'd left off in the car the moment they got inside the elevator, but they didn't have the same good fortune as the previous night and ended up standing in a small crush of people. He was slightly behind her, and she could feel his breath on her neck. It was so distractingly delicious that it was all she could do to hold herself together, and she knew he was doing it on purpose. He was trying to drive her wild and succeeding.

In a move to torture him back, she leaned back slightly, pressing into him just enough to feel his entire body harden against her. His breathing became slightly more ragged, and she felt her stomach twist, her legs lose all strength. By the time the last person left the elevator, she was leaning against him as much for support as anything.

After what felt like ages, they were finally alone. His hands gripped her waist and spun her so she was facing him, and his lips found hers. Before she knew what was happening, she was pressed up against the side of the elevator, his strong body enveloping her. She wrapped her arms around his waist, untucking his shirt so she could feel the skin beneath.

The elevator dinged, causing Aaron to groan, either in excitement that they'd arrived or exasperation that they had to separate at all, or possibly a mixture of both. The sound vibrated deep in his chest, sending more slivers of pleasure through her heightened senses.

She grabbed his arm and slid sideways, making her way out of the elevator and pulling him along with her. His biceps felt large and muscular in her hand, and she felt small and delicate compared to his brute strength. She relished the feeling, as rare as it was for a woman who was pushing five-ten. On the landing she hesitated, unsure of the direction toward his room. He took over then, wrapping his arm back around her waist and moving impatiently.

As he opened the door, she nibbled on his neck, causing him to groan again, and he tightened the arm around her, pulling her into the room with him. The daylight streamed in through the large window, illuminating the massive room. If Jessica had looked around, she would have been impressed at the size of the suite and the view out the window, but she was too busy working on Aaron's shirt. It was the same shirt he'd worn the night before, and she was enjoying pulling it off his body once again.

"I think you might kill me," he said as her hands worked to unbutton the shirt.

"Does that mean you want me to stop?" she asked, already knowing what his answer would be.

"That would *definitely* kill me," he answered, making her smile.

When she'd exposed his chest and placed her hands on his warm, muscular skin, he growled her name and leaned down to kiss her neck. They had backed up against the wall just inside the door, and she was pinned there delectably by his strong body as his hands roved over her still-clothed front, grazing any bare skin he could find until she was panting with anticipation.

She had unfortunately decided to wear a pair of jeans for their outing. "This would be easier if I was wearing a skirt," she lamented, squirming with impatience.

It apparently wasn't an issue for Aaron, however, as he'd unbuttoned and pulled them down all while kissing her neck and down along the scoop neck of her blouse.

Jessica grabbed desperately for the bottom of her shirt and pulled it over her head, catching his chin a little in the process.

He smiled at her as she rushed out a quick apology and raised one eyebrow. "You're sorry because you took your shirt off?"

Before she could respond, his hands had found their way to her bra, undoing the front clasp and teasing her erect nipples. She leaned back against the wall and closed her eyes. "Definitely not sorry," she gasped, making him chuckle.

She moved one foot out of the jeans that were pooled on the floor and wrapped her leg around him, enjoying feeling the jump of his muscles and the added pressure of his fingers as she broke down the last of his control.

He stepped away for only a moment, moving purposely to a drawer to pull out a condom and back before she'd fully gotten out of the last of her clothes. His jeans were still clinging to his body, but the zipper was undone and his penis stood at attention. She kicked off her panties just as he sheathed himself and pressed her once again to the wall. She kissed him long and hard, wrapping her leg around him once again.

"You sure about this?" he asked, the throaty pitch to his voice showing just how much effort it was taking to hold back.

"Absolutely, cowboy," she said without hesitation.

Without moving from their vertical positions, he slid into her, and her mind exploded with pleasure. He pressed harder against her, his hands holding her up as she closed her eyes and gave herself over to the sensations running through her body.

She felt the pressure building inside her, and as she felt the sweet release fluttering through her, she could hear in his moans that he had lost control, as well. They melted together, her passion giving way to satisfaction and a warm fuzzy glow. After a few moments of leaning against the wall, spent, he stepped back and lifted her, carrying her to the couch nearby.

She curled in his arms, happy to feel small and light in his embrace. He set her down carefully, kneeling in front of the couch as he did so. She looked in his eyes and heard her heart thump loudly. It felt as if it was doing somersaults in her chest.

The night before, and even that morning, had been all physical attraction, all raw need. She felt that this was somehow different. It was still physical, but the time together had turned him into a real person for her, not just a fairy-tale mystery man, and that added another dimension to their lovemaking that was wonderful and a little frightening.

If she had met him in New York and spent more than a couple of days with him, she'd definitely have to worry about falling in love with him as well as falling for the unbelievable sex, and she wasn't ready to trust another guy with her whole heart.

It's a good thing we both know this is just one weekend, then, Jessica told herself with a shrug. She could let herself enjoy her time with him, and maybe use it to help mend her self-confidence a little. She had to admit, she had never felt sexier or more confident than when she was with Aaron, and that was huge for her. She'd always felt a little too tall, too closed off, too proper with Russ. This feeling was so very different, and she wanted to soak up every moment of it she could get.

Aaron flopped next to her on the couch, lost in his own thoughts. His jeans were still on, but his torso was bare. For a second, she felt too naked and considered grabbing her clothes, then smiled to herself. Sexy Jessica 2.0 didn't need clothes.

Instead she moved herself until she was stretched out on the couch, her head resting on his lap. "So, what else should we do today?" she asked, enjoying the calm of her body after all the intensity.

He looked down at her, and the edge of his mouth turned up into the small crooked grin she'd started to realize was habitual and incredibly attractive. "What do you want to do?" he asked, giving her the reins.

She stretched, feeling the looseness of her muscles. "Well, the girls are going shopping, but I wasn't planning on joining them. We could go see some other area of Vegas, but I'm a little tired of the glitz."

She left it open, seeing where he would take it. He raised one eyebrow and did his small smile, and she knew he was going to suggest staying in, which brought butterflies to her stomach. This was her one chance, after all. It was like a story from back in wartimes. He'd be shipping out tomorrow, or sometime soon at least, and this was it.

Before he could say anything, his phone started squawking. He rolled his eyes and adjusted himself enough to get the phone out of his back pocket without disturbing her. She appreciated the gesture and settled in, comfortable.

She could feel his eyes grazing her long body stretched out on the couch, naked, and she enjoyed knowing he would like what he saw. He flipped open the phone.

"Jeremiah. What is it?…Damn, I forgot…I know, I just got distracted. I don't think I'll be able to make it. Listen, it's fine, just go without me…Jeremiah, you need to listen to me. Go. With. Out. Me…All right, bye."

"What was that all about?" she asked, curious about the side of the conversation she couldn't hear.

Aaron sighed. "Jeremiah and I are supposed to go to a thing for the rodeo in, like, a half hour. Our ranches are in this competition, and we always have a big bet to see who wins. But it's fine if I don't go. He can just tell me about it later."

She sat up with a slight groan, regretting the need to move from her relaxed position, but she knew that Jeremiah was not happy, and Aaron's friendship with him was far more important than the dalliance they were having. At least, it absolutely should be.

"That's fine, you go," she said in a lighthearted voice that she hoped didn't sound too forced. "You're here with your friend for this reason, right?"

He looked unhappy. "Well, yeah, but—"

"Then you need to go. I'll head out and spend some time with the girls. Cindy will probably have a conniption fit if I just disappear the entire weekend, anyway."

She hopped up and began putting her clothes back on, turning away from him so he couldn't see her disappointment. *It's fine*, she told herself. *I'll see him again tonight. Or tomorrow. Or I won't. That's the way flings go.*

It wasn't very convincing.

Once dressed, she turned toward him. The downcast look on his face would have made her smile if she hadn't felt a bit of the same. He was clearly unhappy she was wearing clothes again, and so was she.

"Go," she reiterated. "Have fun. Meet up with me tonight, if you want."

He looked at her, his eyes flashing, and the thrill of them on her reawakened her senses again. She couldn't believe it to be possible that she wasn't over that yet, but there it was. He said, "You couldn't keep me away."

"Okay, then. What about dinner? Where should we meet?"

"Here."

"Is there a good restaurant in the hotel?"

"Not in a restaurant at the hotel. Here. My room. I'll give you a key card and you can come in whenever you want. I'll be back by eight."

She was surprised he was willing to just give her a key to his room, but she managed to react nonchalantly. "Great. I'll just come by sometime after that."

She laughed internally at her coolness, knowing that she'd have to fight herself to not be at his door at eight o'clock on the dot. He gave her the card, she slipped it in her purse and with a little wave that made him jump off the couch for one last soul-melting kiss, she walked out the door. As soon as it closed behind her, she leaned back against it and breathed in and out deeply.

Jessica couldn't even begin to believe what had happened during the previous twenty-four hours, and she didn't know if she was ecstatic and woozy from it or disappointed that she wouldn't be getting more.

She decided to try and just stay happy. It was temporary and that was all there was to it, she had to remind herself, so there was no point in being disappointed. That would just cause more hurt later, and she wasn't about to let herself get burned on such a short-term arrangement.

Her heart danced as she pictured his reaction when she told him to go, however, and enjoyed the fact that she now knew he actually owned a ranch, despite her previous opinion that real-life details shouldn't be a part of all this.

Realizing she was still leaning against the door, she moved away quickly and headed for the elevators. It would be incredibly awkward if he opened the door and found her still outside his room.

Actually it would probably be wonderful and involve having his arms around her again. Better not to risk that, because she didn't think she could make the right decision again.

7

AARON HADN'T MOVED off the couch since she left. He was still staring at the door, willing her to open it again and come back inside. Finally, after a few minutes, he ran his fingers through his hair, leaned back against the couch and sighed. He didn't know what was going on with him. This woman had him wrapped around her finger somehow, and his tendency to call the shots just completely disappeared when she was around.

He gave her a key. Was that weird? He'd never done that before. He'd met up with plenty of women in Vegas, but he never considered giving them a key to his room, or missing his big competition day of the NFR. Those were two firsts that he hadn't expected.

Now that she was gone, though, there seemed no point in sitting around. Plus, he was going to be late if he didn't get going. He texted Jeremiah and changed, but the image of her head in his lap was still swimming in front of his eyes.

He was going to be sorry to give up Jessica, but he

was glad that the distance and anonymity would stop him from continuing to see her. She was mind-blowing, but he didn't want to hurt her, and he was afraid that it would happen if they spent too much time together.

He had hurt women before, when they wanted more than he was willing to give. He didn't believe in true love and marriage and all that, at least not for him, and it had caused a few rough moments from time to time. That was why he liked to be clear about the situation up front, and what could be more clear than a two-day expiration date?

He exited the hotel room, heading down to Jeremiah's. There was still something about Jessica, though, that was eating at him. There was something under her confidence, her slight hesitancies, that made him think she was unavailable.

He tried to tell himself it didn't matter. She could make her own decisions, and it was one weekend. He shouldn't press the issue or try to get involved. Still, he would never knowingly help someone cheat. He'd need to figure out what to do about that before he saw her in the evening.

Thinking of her walking into his room sent shivers down his spine, and he had to forcibly shift his attention so he could knock on Jeremiah's door and get this whole thing out of the way without any big issues.

Jeremiah answered as soon as he knocked; he'd clearly been waiting for him. Aaron suddenly felt guilty about his treatment of his friend. "Hey, man," he began, "I'm sorry about this whole thing—"

"It's fine," Jeremiah responded coldly.

Aaron felt even worse. He'd been such an ass that he'd made Jeremiah, the perennially happy friend he'd had since grade school, pissed off at him.

They began walking to the elevators. "No, seriously, I'm sorry." He didn't really want to explain but realized he didn't have a choice if he wanted to fix this. "So, I met this girl, and everything just kind of spiraled out of hand. I've got things under control now, though."

That was a lie, he thought. If she called him up, begging him to come back to her, he didn't think he had it in him to say no. Since she had tossed his number, though, it seemed unlikely.

Jeremiah immediately perked up at his explanation. "Yeah? She was that hot, huh?"

Aaron looked into his friend's gleaming eyes and told the truth. "Hotter."

Jeremiah whistled a long, low whistle. "A girl hot enough to make you almost miss our bet. That's a big deal. I'd like to meet her."

As the elevator door dinged shut, Aaron admitted, "You did. She was the girl I talked to outside Sapphire. She was one of the bachelorette-party girls. And she was the one I saw at the airport."

Jeremiah's face showed his incredulity. "Seriously? Those were all the same girl? Some tall brunette, right?"

"More red than brunette, but yeah. The same girl."

"Sounds like fate wants you two together. When's the wedding? She better not wear heels, because as the best man, I shouldn't be shorter than the bride."

For some reason, Jeremiah's teasing bothered Aaron more than it usually would have. A surge of annoyance flashed through him, but he managed to keep his voice steady. "You know it's not like that. It's just a weekend thing. I don't even know where she lives."

Jeremiah shrugged. "She's from New York, probably, if she's with the bachelorette party. They're all from there. Marilyn wouldn't stop talking about it. Apparently it's the best city ever. It was worth listening to her, though."

As Jeremiah continued talking about his date in more or less graphic detail, Aaron drifted into his own thoughts. Now he knew where she was from. Was that really so bad? He couldn't expect them to keep everything about themselves quiet, and he had already mentioned Texas. He'd felt stupid after letting it slip, but she had to have guessed before he said anything. He was at the rodeo, after all.

He could see her walking around New York. She'd be able to handle that big city with her cool confidence and powerful stare.

In a way, it was good to know where she called home. She was from a huge city thousands of miles away from where he lived. There wasn't even the slightest possibility they'd run into each other later. Good, because thinking he might bump into her one day would likely drive him crazy.

Aaron tried to refocus his mind, to listen to Jeremiah. He'd been a pretty lousy friend before, and didn't want something as little as a weekend fling to get between them. Even if the woman in question was stunning. And interesting. And completely captivating. And it didn't *feel* little.

He needed to pull himself together.

Finally Jeremiah stopped talking as they walked through the noisy casino and out into the fresh air. The rodeo was held at the Thomas and Mack Center on the university campus, just a couple of blocks away. They made their way along the sidewalks filled with people in cowboy hats and boots, all heading to the same destination.

He became lost in deliciously inappropriate thoughts about what he might do that evening to surprise Jessica. He wanted to make her smile. Jeremiah's voice cut through his thoughts, startling him. "Is this all because of that girl, or is there something else going on?"

Aaron was bewildered. He knew he'd been a little distracted, but was he acting that strange? "Nothing's going on. Why?"

"You've been acting really weird since you met her. Not in a good way. Have you spent more than five minutes since you saw her without thinking about her?"

Aaron paused for a minute, embarrassed.

"Yeah, I didn't think so. That's dangerous, man. You don't want some girl taking over your life, especially if you live, like, three thousand miles away from her. You don't want to do anything stupid."

Aaron nodded. Jeremiah was right. "Yeah. I've been too distracted. It's just a fun weekend thing. When we leave on Tuesday, I'll be getting on the plane without a second glance. Sorry if I've been a jerk."

Jeremiah slapped him on the back and grinned. "It's no problem. I just don't want you to abandon your life, sell the land and run off to New York or anything." He laughed at his joke.

Aaron chuckled, too, a knot twisting in his gut. He'd never do something that stupid. Leaving his whole life for a girl could only end in disaster, and he knew that. He'd seen it happen before. His mom had been a wreck when his dad went running off after true love, and look how well that worked out for him.

No, Aaron knew that "love" meant giving up your happiness, your independence, your life. There was no way he was going to let anything like that happen to him. He was just having fun with Jessica. After he went back home, he would continue on his own as he'd been doing for years.

He liked his life just the way it was. It got a little lonely sometimes, eating dinner alone or with a few buddies, but there were enough women who knew his boundaries and were happy to keep him company for a while to break up the monotony.

The thought of those women left a weird taste in his mouth, and the "fun" he'd been having with them suddenly seemed less fun.

Aaron walked beside Jeremiah into the arena the city had prepared for the many competitions and events included in the annual rodeo. It felt like a football stadium, huge and crowded, but the smell was definitely rodeo. Hay and horses and dirt. That smell meant home to him.

Better to focus on the here and now, to enjoy the competitions, than to think about his choices. He didn't like the way it felt to think about all that other stuff. It was better to just not worry about the future. Everything would go back to normal when he got out of Vegas.

It was impossible to feel normal in Vegas, he told himself.

As if to solidify that fact, a buxom fake blonde tapped him on the shoulder and smiled widely at him. The bad taste in his mouth intensified as he recognized Olivia, his semiregular rodeo companion. His mind went blank, and he couldn't think of anything to say to her. Luckily she was the one to break the silence.

"Aaron! I can't believe you haven't even texted me. You have to have been in town for at least a day or two, right?" He didn't answer, but evidently she wasn't looking for a reply. "Let's go find your seat and watch the fun. I can spend a little while with you before I have to get back to my group. Where's Jeremiah?"

That was one he could answer. He pointed to his friend standing near the stairs that led to their seats. He was talking to a group of guys Aaron recognized from previous years, probably telling them how well his team would be doing this year. Olivia bounced over to Jeremiah and gave him a friendly hug. Aaron couldn't hear what she was saying, but he could tell it was something bubbly and enthusiastic. He knew he should walk up to them, but he didn't particularly want to.

Over her shoulder, Jeremiah looked at him and raised his eyebrows. It was a small gesture, but enough to let Aaron know what his friend was thinking. What was he going to do about her? Aaron shrugged in return. He just didn't know. She wasn't the kind of woman to get hurt feelings, but he didn't want to have to explain anything about Jessica if he didn't have to. It wouldn't make any sense if he tried, anyway.

And there was no way Olivia would be coming back to his room that evening. After all, Jessica was going to be there. Well, was probably going to be there. He didn't even have her phone number, so she could just not show up.

He felt a second of cold panic at the thought of her disappearing without a word, but it was gone in a flash. She was going to come back. He'd seen it in her eyes when he gave her the key card.

Even if she wasn't, Olivia was really too fake for him. Her hair, her boobs, her laugh, even her personality were all fake. He wanted a real woman. One who wasn't afraid to be seen without makeup, who said what she honestly thought, who actually thought things. He wasn't sure why he'd spent so much time around Olivia in the past.

He watched as she hooked her arm through Jeremiah's, allowing him to usher her toward their seats. Jeremy looked back at him and gestured with his head toward the stairs that led to the rows of seats. Apparently Aaron had hung back long enough.

He slowly walked toward them, following their progress without attempting to catch up. He didn't want to be there. Back in his room, with Jessica resting her head on his lap, he'd felt relaxed and happy. Now he was dreading the next few hours of small talk and smiling as Olivia flung herself against him every time something happened in the arena.

He knew he couldn't abandon Jeremiah there—he

had some decency—but he'd have to come up with something to tell Olivia so she wouldn't think she was going back to the hotel with him. By the time he got to his and Jeremiah's seats, Olivia was already in a full-blown story about something exciting and amazing that had happened to her, and Aaron had to keep from rolling his eyes. She was also sitting in his seat, leaving him to sit in somebody else's until they arrived or Olivia decided to leave. He hoped it was the latter, and soon.

He sat down. Olivia only noticed enough to flash him a smile and turn herself slightly so her story was directed at both of them, but she didn't seem to notice his mood.

What was wrong with him? He'd always known she was a little shallow and not exactly a person you'd want to spend hours talking to, but he'd never thought of her in this "dear God, get me away from her" way. He didn't want to think about what that might mean for his life back at home. Some of the women he spent time around were interesting and could keep up their end of a conversation, but most of those had settled down with some other guy and moved on.

Actually even quite a few of the less-interesting ones had, too. Now that he was in his late twenties, the pool of eligible women who weren't looking for a serious relationship had dwindled to a muddy puddle. How had he not noticed that?

He angled himself away from the chattering woman next to him and focused on the show, hoping she'd take the hint that he wasn't interested without making him come up with some excuse or shooting her down completely—knowing Olivia's personality as well as he did, though, he doubted it would work. Catching on wasn't one of her strong suits. And if he was going to break things off with her, he wanted to do it somewhere private, which just wasn't possible at the moment. The place was packed and getting more crowded every second.

"Isn't that hilarious, Aaron?" she asked, gripping his arm for a moment.

He smiled at her and nodded, trying his best not to be a total dick.

Below them, in the center of the arena, a few workers were preparing for the first competition of the evening, checking the hard-packed dirt floor for anything that might hurt the riders or animals. Bull riding was the main event, the last of the evening, but before that there was the bareback bronc competition, and then team roping. What he and Jeremiah were there for.

Their teams had been preparing for this all year, and whatever Jeremiah said about his team, Aaron knew his pair of riders were the best. He could picture them, working in perfect synchronicity to rope their steer, the header's rope looping around the steer's horns a split second before the heeler tossed his around the steer's back legs, tightening them at the same moment. They had been working together for years, and moved as one person, as if they were in each other's minds.

With any luck, they would make it into the top three, maybe even get first place if the horses were steady enough to try the trick they'd been working on the past couple of months. A tenth of a second could mean the difference between a win and a loss here.

Aaron could still hear Olivia chattering away, but he kept his attention on the arena, watching the first competitor mount the bronco being held still behind the gate. In just a few seconds, he would be let loose, and the cowboy would need to hold on for eight seconds with only one hand on the horse that was trying to buck him off.

A snap of a latch and the gate was open. The bronco ran the arena, using his entire body to try to knock the man off his back. Olivia gasped and clutched at his arm, hiding her eyes against his shoulder.

Aaron pictured Jessica there beside him. He could imagine it perfectly, her body tilted forward as she studied the movements of the bronco and the rider, working to figure out what tiny adjustments the cowboy would need to make in order to stay on and get the highest number of points.

It was foolish thinking, and he tried to put it out of his head. What would ever make her interested in watching rodeo events? She was from New York— rodeo probably seemed silly and pointless to her. If in some alternative universe she went with him to a rodeo, she would hate it, most likely.

He couldn't get himself to believe that, though. Her competitive nature was too strong for her to dismiss it all out of hand, and she just seemed like the type of person who was interested in anything that could be seen as a puzzle. That was what he always liked about these competitions himself.

The buzzer sounded and the cowboy's eight-second ride was over. Rodeo clowns swarmed the arena, helping the cowboy gain control of the horse.

"Not a bad ride," Jeremiah commented over Olivia's head.

Aaron agreed. The man's style was too choppy for a score much higher than the mid-eighties, but it was decent. The people cheered and shouted, and the announcer's voice boomed as the next rider climbed into the chute. Olivia continued to clutch at his arm. He wished the owner of his seat would get there quickly.

She squeezed his arm a little tighter and talked to him in a whisper that could be heard by anyone in a five-foot radius. "Do you want to make some plans for when all this is done? I'm free all night."

She smiled at him. He knew that even just the year before he'd thought she had a sexy seductive smile, but it just looked too forced to be intriguing. For the first time since meeting her nearly five years ago, he wondered what she was really like under all the layers of show.

He didn't want to hurt her, but he couldn't think of anything to say. She watched him expectantly as he racked his mind for a response.

He needed to say something, but nothing even halfway decent came to him. Finally he just said, "I can't," while he tried to decide the nicest way to tell her that it wasn't going to happen.

She frowned, but perked up after a second or two. "Okay, well, let me know if you're still in town tomorrow and maybe we'll be able to spend time together.

It would be a shame to let a whole year go by before we…catch up."

He had to explain to her that they wouldn't be "catching up" this year, or any future ones for that matter. "Yeah, so Olivia…" he began, trying to find the right words.

But before he could say anything more, she hopped up. "Great! Just text me whenever. I'm going to head over to my seat. I'll see you boys later."

He watched her go, dumbfounded. Maybe it was for the best, though. He'd learned in the past that she could get mean—and loud—when she was sad or angry, and she tended to take any rejection pretty personally, so letting her down in public was probably not the best idea. He needed to find a way to talk to her privately without making her expect sex. That was a tall order.

He'd have to figure out how to deal with the situation without hurting her or making her think they might still get together someday. Stringing women along had never been how he did things, and he wasn't about to start now.

This was a very strange situation for him. He'd never felt wrong about his relationship with a woman and wanted to end it without having an actual reason. Even though he wasn't planning on marrying any of the women he spent time with or anything like that, he had his own moral code. He didn't lie to them about his intentions or expectations of their relationship. He wasn't going to hold anyone back from living their lives.

There was nothing he could do about it at that moment, so he tried to shut off his mind and just watch the event. The only thing he couldn't get out of his head, couldn't stop even if he wanted to, was an image of a beautiful woman with green eyes smiling at him.

He just couldn't let that go, could he?

8

JESSICA SAT ON a bench, letting the other girls run into the nearest store without her. She was exhausted from following them around, and they'd been going through the mall as if it was a battlefield and they were all determined to leave victorious. She was pretty sure she was a casualty.

She just wanted to go back to her room. Or better yet, Aaron's room. She wasn't spending any extra money; after all, she was still working on figuring out her living arrangement when they got back to New York, and no matter what apartment she managed to find, it would be so expensive that she'd need every penny she had. Her mom and dad wouldn't allow her to move back home—they said they didn't want her underfoot, but she knew they wanted her to have as normal a life as she could despite her dad's illness.

So she waited on the bench, picturing other possible places to live. It broke her heart to think of it, but someday soon her father would pass, and once that happened,

Jessica didn't think she could stay in New York any longer. She had been considering moving before she met Russ, but then they got together and he couldn't leave the city, so she stayed. By the time their relationship ended, her dad was already sick. Her family kept encouraging her to go out and see the world, and maybe someday she would. As an editor, she could live anywhere. Like LA or San Francisco or Florida, or even a ranch in Texas.

Nope. No ranches. She gave herself a mental slap. She could already tell that leaving Vegas and her newfound pleasures would be difficult. If she started fantasizing about something that could never happen, it would only leave her hurting, and she *refused* to allow that.

She was a little worried about what it would be like to be home and alone once again. She was very quickly becoming addicted to Aaron's bed—not that they'd ever actually made it to his bed—and she had very briefly considered not going back to see him at all. Except she knew that *that* wasn't going to happen. He'd invited her back, and she just didn't have it in her to say no.

Cindy walked out of the store, no new bags added to her already-weighty haul, and sat next to her. Jessica looked at her in surprise. "What's going on? Couldn't find anything you liked?"

Cindy shrugged. "I wanted to chat for a second. You've been weird and distracted."

Jessica was about to argue, and then realized that her friend was right. And she could picture the cause of it in glorious detail.

As if Cindy could read her thoughts, she turned her whole body toward Jessica and looked her straight in the eye. "You aren't falling in love with him or anything colossally stupid like that, right?"

Jessica would have laughed, but the concern on her friend's face made it clear she wasn't joking. "Cindy, no. Absolutely not. I'm just having a fun time. Letting loose a little or something."

Cindy seemed skeptical. "Fun's great, but you've been walking around all day in your own little wonderland, and that smile on your lips seems like it's more than just an 'I had awesome sex' smile."

"An 'I had awesome sex' smile? What exactly does that look like?"

"It's the smile Marilyn's been wearing all day. Yours isn't the same."

Jessica didn't know what to say to that. This conversation was far out of her realm of normalcy. "And mine's different?"

"Yep. Yours is a cute 'I had awesome sex with a guy I want to marry and have babies with' smile."

Jessica couldn't believe how serious Cindy looked. As if this wasn't all crazy nonsense from her imagination. "Maybe my 'I had awesome sex' smile is different than Marilyn's."

Cindy would not be deterred. "All I'm saying is that you seem like you're falling for this guy despite the fact that it's an impossible relationship."

"I'm not. I swear I'm not. I've been hurt enough to know that anything more than a fun time with this guy isn't going to happen. I don't even want it to happen. I saw him outside the strip club with his arms around two women, drunk and staring wide-eyed at their boobs. Trust me, I'm not going to forget that."

Cindy looked slightly mollified, though not completely convinced. "Well, just don't lose your head, okay? It's going to end soon enough, and then you'll have to get back to life at home. Maybe you can start dating again. Get yourself back on the market."

"Yeah, maybe," Jessica replied, but the thought only dropped her mood. Dating meant obnoxious strangers, uncomfortable pauses and awkward moments as she said good-night and spent the rest of the evening alone.

Dates had never gone well for her, whether she was going out with men from bars or guys from dating websites or on blind dates set up by sympathetic friends. Since she worked at home, those were the only ways she met eligible men, and none of them had worked out. Even Russ, by far the best dating experience she'd had, got off to a rocky start and ended horribly.

She could see that her friend was still concerned. "Cindy, it's really nothing. I'm just smiling an 'I had awesome sex' smile, and I'm going to leave with no hurt feelings. I promise."

The amount of force in her voice finally got Cindy to nod, accepting, and walk back into the store. Jessica leaned back, hoping she was telling the truth. She definitely wasn't going to fall in love with Aaron, but she couldn't say that it would be easy to tear herself away from something so amazing. If only he'd been the stupid sex maniac she'd assumed he was when she saw him at the strip club. But no, dammit. He had to be sweet and like *Harry Potter*.

After what seemed like an eternity, the girls had exhausted themselves and were ready to get back to the hotel so they could rest a little before dinner. Jessica was happy to see that it was nearly seven, and went to her room to dress. She was tired, and her eyes were telling her that she needed more sleep than she'd gotten the past two nights, but her mind was whirling with visions of Aaron.

In her room, she pulled everything out of her bag and considered each item carefully. She had two sexy dresses, both borrowed from Cindy and both he'd already seen, two dresses she had brought that looked decidedly frumpy next to the others, the pair of jeans she'd been wearing all day and a few blouses.

She wasn't very happy with her options. She liked the way she'd looked in the dresses, and it felt nice to be a hotter version of herself, but she didn't want to wear one of them and be stuck with that as her only clothing the next day.

Planning on staying at his room sent a thrill down her spine. Yes, she was tired, but she'd gladly give up mental awareness and a little bit of sanity for another night like the one she'd just had. So, with that in mind, the jeans were really the best bet. But what to wear with them? None of the shirts she brought were good enough.

She wanted to be surprising and erotic, and her normal clothes certainly did not fit that mold. Then she looked at her New York coat hanging over the back of a chair, where she'd tossed it and forgotten about it in the pleasant weather. She smiled.

On the short taxi ride to his hotel, she couldn't stop fidgeting and felt as if she couldn't catch her breath. Her stomach was alive with a fluttery feeling she couldn't stop. Not butterflies, though. Butterflies would indicate that she was nervous, as if this were a date or something. There was no reason to be nervous because it was all just a fun adventure and nothing more.

She'd purposely waited at her hotel until eight even though she was ready to go a half hour before. She tried to work a little, but it was impossible to edit anything. She couldn't absorb any of the words, let alone full paragraphs of text. She'd assumed she wouldn't get much work done over the weekend, but she'd start getting harried emails if she couldn't get something sent out soon.

Thoughts of work drifted immediately to the back of her mind as she got close to Aaron's hotel. There were too many other things to think about. Like Aaron's hands touching her. That occupied a large part of her mental real estate.

Now that she was on her way, though, her thoughts turned anxious and the taxi ride felt far too short. She almost begrudgingly left the cab and paid the driver. This was one of the craziest things she'd ever done, but her nerves quickly turned to excitement as she looked at the Hard Rock's glass doors. This was her chance to be daring and sexy, and she was going to take advantage of it. She took a deep breath and walked quickly through the casino. In the elevator, she checked her phone for the time. Twelve after eight.

Not exactly what someone would call fashionably late, and most girls would chide her for looking too eager, but that was the best she could do. Another twenty minutes of waiting around would have been impossible torture if what was waiting for her inside his room was anything like what it had been earlier.

She was finally on his floor. One deep, slow breath, and she was in front of the door. The edges of the key card felt sharp against her palm, but the thought of actually using it felt absurd. Storming into his room without knocking did not sound daring and sexy, it sounded rude, even if he had given her a key. Still, he gave it to her. Clearly he wanted her to use it.

She was standing outside his door, staring at the key card and trying to decide what to do, when the door suddenly opened. Her heart jumped and she stepped back quickly.

Aaron was standing there, looking as handsome as he had been in the fantasies she'd been playing out in her head for the past several hours. He smiled at her. She was still shocked. "How did you know I was out here?"

"I heard the elevator ding a minute ago, and then steps up to the door, and then your bag or something hit the door. It wasn't too hard to solve the mystery. Hi. I was waiting for you."

His words and that cute-as-hell crooked smile made her melt for just a second before she pulled it back together. She told herself it was because he was being sexy, not cute. There was a big difference, and all she wanted was sexy.

He held the door open and she walked in. On the

dining room table—his suite was ridiculously big, she finally noticed—there were several platters with silver domes on top. He'd clearly ordered them room service for dinner.

A thrill went down her spine again. He definitely wasn't planning on them leaving the room for the rest of the evening. While she was standing there looking around, he closed the door and came up behind her. She suddenly found herself wrapped in his arms, his scent and his voice as he whispered, "Totally not worth it. I could have been here all day. I never should've let you talk me into going."

She leaned into him, smiling as his warm breath tickled the back of her neck. "How'd your ranch do?"

He pulled back a little and loosened his grip. She immediately regretted saying anything that would cause him to stop holding her, but he just readjusted enough to turn her toward him. "Actually we got second place. We've only ever gotten up to fifth before, so it was a pretty big deal. We're celebrating tonight."

Her heart dropped a little, but she did her best to hide the disappointment. "Oh, well, if you need to go out with your team or whatever, that's fine. I'm pretty tired and could use some sleep, anyway."

He leaned his head back and laughed, and the rich golden notes bounced around the room like a bell chiming. "Not them. We. You and me we. I got some champagne and we can celebrate up here. I don't think we need the other guys for what I've got in mind."

Her blood rushed hot through her. She wanted to curl up in his arms, lean her head against him and breathe deeply, just smelling him and enjoying his warmth and closeness, but that would probably seem a little too relationship-ish. Instead she turned back around and began unzipping her heavy jacket. "Will you take my coat?"

"Sure. That's a pretty thick jacket for such a warm evening. Why—"

She smiled to herself. Without looking at him, she could tell that the coat had been a very good idea. Now that it was in his hands, she was standing in front of him in nothing but jeans and bare skin. Finally, after the silence had dragged on for longer than she'd expected, she turned her head to the side, still keeping her back facing him.

He was standing there holding the jacket, and the death grip he had on it and the expression on his face made her stand a little straighter, letting him soak it all in. Finally he let out a long breath and a low, half-whispered "Wow."

She couldn't help laughing, and suddenly his arms were back around her and she was again spun in his direction. She marveled once more at how light and insubstantial she was in his strong arms. It made her feel almost petite. Then he was kissing her, and her mind stopped thinking altogether. His lips brushed against the corner of her mouth, then her jaw, then began moving slowly down toward her bare shoulder, getting more intense as he went until he was lightly biting at the base of her neck.

As his hands curved along her stomach, she sighed, joy washing through her. Any stress or anxiety she had felt that day, all her exhaustion, fell away. He smiled back, and she knew he felt the same. How could letting a near stranger touch and kiss her feel so right? She didn't know, but she wasn't about to start trying to find out. She only knew that she was deliriously happy, and she hadn't felt anything close to that in a very, very long time.

She lost herself in his caresses and allowed her hands to wander along his chest and down to where his penis throbbed beneath the heavy denim of his pants.

They somehow made it to his bed without her noticing exactly how they'd gotten there.

Her legs pressed against the bed behind her, and she trembled with excitement. The heat raced through her veins as she allowed herself to fall backward onto the overly large comforter. She looked up at the man above her, the mysterious cowboy with the piercing blue gaze that was focused completely on her, and was amazed that she was experiencing this moment.

Even if she never saw him again—she felt a twinge of sadness at the thought, but ignored it—she'd have this memory trapped inside her forever. She'd always be able to keep at least a little part of it alive in her mind. Even in the cold and bitterness of New York she'd have a knot of warmth.

She didn't realize she was grinning until he smiled back. He lowered himself so his upper body engulfed hers, though his bottom half was still off the bed. He kissed the corner of her lips, then fully on her mouth, his tongue diving inside, flicking against her own in a way that felt like so much more than a kiss. She wrapped her arms around his shoulders and lifted herself into him, giving herself fully over to the kiss. It was long and grew in intensity as they pressed their bodies inexorably closer.

Just when she felt as though she could wait no longer for him, he separated himself from her by a few inches, enough to whisper, "You're amazing, Jessica."

Her heart skipped, and she ignored the small voice in the back of her mind telling her she was getting in too deep. Instead she whispered back, "I want you, Aaron."

Slowly, almost agonizingly, he removed the last of his clothes and hers, sliding his hands over every inch of bare skin he revealed on her body until she was shaking from anticipation and the desperate need to have him. When they were both fully undressed and he had sheathed himself, and she was sure that he would slide inside her, he instead knelt on the floor beside the bed, pulling her gently toward the edge.

His hands worked their way up from her ankles up to her thighs, until she opened herself to him, revealing her wetness. His fingers brushed across her, and her back arched at the soft touch, the anticipation engulfing her. When his fingers were replaced by his mouth, her body released, sending a rush through her, and she cried out as it flooded her.

Only then did he bring himself to her, pressing the lengths of their bodies together, sinking his girth deep into her warm folds. As he penetrated her, his hand found hers on the bed, and they slowly rocked back and forth, enjoying the warmth of the moment.

Almost imperceptibly, the speed increased and his

thrusts intensified, until she was brought again to the brink, and together their bodies reached a crescendo, leaving them both gasping, his weight pressing her into the bed's soft coverings.

She didn't move, eyes closed, enjoying the weight of him. Instead of feeling stifled or pinned down, which she would have expected, she felt protected and co-cooned by him. One arm was wrapped around him, her hand slowly running up and down his back. The other was still clasped in his.

After a time that felt like both a delicious eternity and the briefest of moments, Aaron shifted himself until he was beside her, leaning on one elbow so he could look into her face. "I've never been to New York before. I think I should definitely go see it. Soon."

Her eyes flew open wide and she looked at him, a little taken aback, but also pleased despite herself. Her thoughts ran quickly, trying to come up with something appropriate to say, but one question rose to the front: *How does he know where I live?* She was positive she'd never mentioned it.

As if he could see what she was thinking, he shrugged. "I was talking to Jeremiah, and when I said I didn't know where you're from, he told me. Apparently your friend is pretty chatty."

For a second, she didn't know who he was talking about; the only friend he'd met of hers was Cindy, and she certainly didn't spend any time around Jeremiah. Then she realized he was talking about Marilyn. She was kind of her friend now.

He really didn't know anything about her. That was

a good thing for a single weekend, but was he asking to be something more than that? Or was he just looking for a friend with benefits whom he could hop on a plane to see occasionally?

She didn't think she could do that.

Looking up at his body and into his eyes, she felt the pull of attraction. She wanted to see him again, but that could get dangerous very quickly, and she was not about to set herself up for more heartache. Jessica knew she had to make the safer choice, but she didn't know how she could say no to seeing him again when all of her screamed out yes.

He was still looking at her, waiting patiently for an answer. She had to say something. "I don't know."

Neither of the sides within her was happy with that, but it was all she could say. The worst thing, though, was the look in Aaron's eyes. Even though he put on a half smile and nodded, accepting her nondecision, his eyes dimmed with disappointment. She had to say something. She tried to explain herself.

"I like you, Aaron, and this weekend has been amazing, but I just don't see that working out. I can't be some girl you hook up with every once in a while when you come into town. I'm definitely not looking for a relationship, and I don't think you are, either. That doesn't leave us with a lot of options, does it?"

She wanted him to agree with her, yet she also hoped that he could somehow figure out a way to make the impossible work. He just nodded and leaned back on the bed, his eyes no longer digging into hers. She stared at the ceiling, wishing she could make him understand. Her thoughts started spilling out in a rush.

"Up until a few months ago, I was living with a guy named Russ. We'd been together for two years and had been talking about getting married. When I found out he was—"

She broke off, reliving the feelings of that day months before. She cleared her throat a couple of times and continued.

"When I found out he was cheating on me, it hurt me more than I can say. It almost destroyed me to see my life crumble like that. I can see now that it was really the best thing, that it would have been far worse if I hadn't found out, but that doesn't mean I'm okay."

Jessica sat up and looked at him. His full attention was on her. She tried to lighten the mood, which had gotten far too heavy for her liking. "At least I know how screwed up I am, right?"

He didn't laugh. Didn't even smile. She said, "This needs to stay a fun once-in-a-lifetime thing. This isn't the real me, you know," she said, blushing, but didn't look away. "I'd only ever slept with Russ before you came along, and I don't plan on being with another guy until I'm ready to trust someone again."

Their eyes were locked, and she saw his eyes darken and contract, but she wasn't sure what he was feeling, whether he was angry or sad or contemptuous. After the silence had lingered until she was considering getting up and leaving, he finally responded, "You don't trust me."

She sighed, hesitant to tell the truth. "I barely know

you, and the second time I ever saw you, you were draped across multiple women. I'm not saying that's a bad thing," she added, seeing he was about to argue. "I'm just saying we're different, and I don't think we could ever find a situation we're both happy with. If you were never planning on having sex with those women and are an innocent guy who didn't sleep around before you met me, you can tell me and I'll change my opinion. Until then, I have to leave this as a wonderful weekend I'll remember the rest of my life."

After a moment, he shut his mouth, and she nodded. The part of her hoping for some response went into hiding deep inside her. She had her answer, and it was time to move past it. She said, "Can we just forget this happened? We don't have much time left here. I'm leaving the day after tomorrow, early in the morning, and I want to spend that time with you, if that's okay."

She waited hopelessly, knowing her magic weekend had turned back into a pumpkin and her prince was gone forever.

Aaron sat up beside her, placed his hand on her cheek and guided her face toward his. He kissed the tracks that were left by the tears she hadn't realized she'd shed, and then he kissed her passionately on the mouth, tantalizing her with his tongue until she was nearly crying again, though she didn't know why.

In his quietest voice, he said, "One wonderful weekend, then. We better make the most of it."

He kissed her again, then stood up, smiling his carefree, jaunty half smile. She noticed it didn't fully reach his eyes, but she wasn't going to demand more. "But first, we need to eat something. Have you had anything?"

As she shook her head, he went to the closet and pulled out two long white robes. He slid one over himself, and she felt a sting of remorse as he tied the belt around his waist. She wasn't in the mood to eat, but he held out the robe to her, so she got off the bed and allowed him to place it on her and tie it around her with gentle fingers.

The mood in the room wasn't going to shift as easily as he seemed to hope, but Aaron clearly wasn't giving up. He grabbed her hand and pulled her to the dining table and began revealing dish after dish. "I wasn't sure what you would want to have for dinner, so I got a few very different things. Eat what you want. I'll take care of the rest. We have a steak, medium rare, a salad with dressings and whatnot on the side and a gourmet pizza margherita from a little restaurant down the street."

The last one caught her attention. "Wait, this wasn't just room service? You actually went out and got a pizza?"

He chuckled good-naturedly, and his expression became a little more genuine. "I'm paying for two suites in this hotel and have yet to destroy any expensive property. When I asked the front desk where I could get quality pizza, they practically fell over themselves to make sure I got what I wanted. I think they're used to guests that are a little more high-maintenance than I am."

She laughed, and some of the anxiety that had been gathering inside her over the previous several minutes eased. She looked around at the funky-but-elegant décor, imagining the type of characters who would rent the Hard Rock suites. Compared to the disasters she could envision, Aaron must have been a godsend for the hotel.

He grinned widely at her, and she felt the tension in the room break completely. "Eat anything you like. It's been sitting awhile now, so I can either heat stuff up in the kitchen or order some more. Just as long as you eat something."

Once the stress of the situation dissipated, she realized that she was in fact quite hungry. She picked up the steak and the pizza, took them into the kitchen— which was bigger than the kitchen in her New York apartment—and began reheating them. As she did so, she called back over her shoulder, "You seemed to have forgotten that I'm not as tiny as most girls, so I'm afraid we might run out of food here if your appetite is anything like what it was at breakfast. I'm not going to be eating that salad, but I'll eat either the steak or the pizza, or I'll share fifty-fifty."

She looked back at him and saw that he was already walking toward the phone. She felt pleased as she waited for the food to heat and knew that things were back on track. There was still a tiny knot of discontent within her, but she managed to ignore it.

9

AARON HUNG UP the hotel's phone after ordering a second steak. He liked that Jessica wasn't shy about her appetite, and internally berated himself for forgetting that she had eaten almost as much at breakfast as he did. To be fair, he had hardly noticed the food on the table that morning. He had been listening to her and watching her lithe movements so intently that there hadn't been any mental force left to pay attention to something as inconsequential as food.

He looked back over at her working in the kitchen and felt his spirits lift. He still had a tornado of emotions inside, but it felt as though he had a good grasp on them now, at least. He was embarrassed that he'd been shot down, disappointed that he'd never see her again, chagrined at how perfectly she'd pegged him and happy that she was still in his room, willing to spend at least this time with him.

He didn't know exactly what made him decide to talk to her about seeing each other again, except that their time together was so incredible he couldn't imagine her saying no. At some point when he was getting his room ready for her, the idea of visiting her in New York and spending hours in bed together, then walking around the huge city he'd only seen in movies seemed great. It would be sexy and fun and enjoyable for them both.

Her response had completely shocked him. Once he heard her story he understood, but that didn't stop him from feeling a little wounded. Women rarely turned him down, and when they did it was simply something to shrug off. This time was different.

In fact, he felt different enough about Jessica that it was probably for the best that she didn't want to see him again. He was getting far too hung up on her. Now that he knew without a doubt that things were over at the end of his stay in Vegas, he could just soak up the time he had without considering the possibility of creating some kind of arrangement for the future.

Aaron wanted to make sure there wouldn't be awkwardness between them for the rest of the time they had, but he wasn't positive how he could do that. He sat at the table and watched her. She was leaning against the counter, waiting for the microwave to finish. Her bare feet and long legs stretching down beneath the robe made her look at home even though she was in a strange kitchen in a hotel suite.

He spoke, trying to break the silence and get them on some solid footing. "What are your plans for tomorrow? Do you have anything you need to do with your friends?"

He'd given her an out if she didn't want to see him

again, but he hoped she didn't take it. She turned toward him, and the spark that alighted every time he looked in her eyes blazed up once more. She tilted her head, as if thinking. "We're supposed to be going to one last celebratory dinner that I should definitely go to, but I'm not sure what time it'll be. Probably around seven or eight. Beyond that, they're all shopping the whole time, and I'd prefer not to go through that again. Our flight leaves around eleven in the morning the next day."

So she was still willing to spend the majority of her time with him. He could accept that, even if there was an expiration date. "Great. If you don't mind, I've got some ideas of things to do tomorrow. You'll be back in plenty of time for your dinner."

"Back? We're going away somewhere?"

He nodded. He could tell she was curious, but he didn't say anything else. He just smiled at her, enjoying the moment. Finally she asked, "Are you going to tell me where?"

"Nope."

She laughed. "Okay, then. I guess I'll have to wait and see."

"Yep."

They looked at each other, enjoying the moment. The knock on the door broke the companionable silence, and he tore his eyes from hers. "It's room service. Now we should have enough for a proper dinner."

As he walked over to the door and got the rest of their meal, he could hear her in the kitchen. By the time he was back, the table was in order, the salad shunted to the side, the steak meal in front of her and the small fancy pizza in the middle, both steaming hot. He set the new portion in front of his own spot. "Are you sure you don't want the new one?"

"I like mine more medium well, so this is perfect now. I don't like my cow while it's still mooing. You go ahead."

They sat down and began eating. While they demolished their steaks and even shared some of the pizza, they chatted about their lives. The barrier was broken, and talking about what went on in the real world felt natural. He listened to her talk about her job as an editor and her quest for a new apartment.

"I've looked at a dozen places, and they're all either way out of my price range, somewhere a murderer would live while he hid from the cops or a place I would have to share with a roommate. Nothing against other people, but Cindy's about the only one I can stand in small quarters for very long, and her apartment is huge."

We seem to get along fine.

He pushed the thought away, but there was just enough of a pause for him to wonder if she thought the same thing. That was *not* Vegas-fling kind of thinking, though, so he brought the conversation back to safer territory. "How did you and Cindy manage to get such a great apartment?"

"It belongs to Cindy's parents. They have a ton of money. We pay rent, but it's nothing close to what we should be paying for that kind of space."

"Have you ever thought about leaving the city?" he asked, purely to keep the conversation moving. It in no way affected him either way.

He tried to ignore how false that excuse was.

She paused. "I've considered it, but I'm going to stay in New York for now. Maybe I'll move someday."

She was holding back something. He wanted to ask, but if she didn't want to talk about it, that was fair. This wasn't a long-term relationship or anything.

That thought bugged him more than he wanted to admit.

She pointed her fork at him. "And what about you? You have a ranch, but I don't really know what that means. Are there cows or something? Do you spit tobacco into spittoons after you've rustled up some cattle thieves?"

Her questions amused him to no end. "Is there anything you know about ranches that you didn't get from a movie?"

"Well, I've read *Of Mice and Men*. It's one of my favorite books. Is it more like that? Wrestling grain bags and all that? Are you the owner's son who picks on Lennie and gets what's coming to him? You don't seem like a Curley, but that's all I've got to base my guesses on."

"Yeah, you've clearly read that book too many times. Ranches aren't exactly like that anymore. I've got some people who work for me, but they come to work every day like normal people. No bunkhouses or anything like that."

Her smile widened and she raised one eyebrow. "Sounds like I'm not the only one who's read that book too many times."

He smiled back. "Yes, but that's not where all my working knowledge of ranches come from. I don't base my entire concept of New York on *Catcher in the Rye* or something."

"Well, then tell me about it and stop getting off topic. I've been waiting for, like, five minutes to hear about ranches."

God, he loved talking to her. She could add fun twists to any conversation, it seemed, and her dry humor was incredible. "There is a small garden with vegetables, but that's just a side thing because going to the store is a pain and I thought it would be fun. We mostly do horses. We give lessons and enter competitions, but most of the income is from breeding and selling."

She gestured at the opulent room around them. "It's so weird to me that selling horses earns enough to let you get the fancy suite when you go to Vegas. Do you always get to live the high life, or is this just a once-a-year thing?"

He never really liked talking about his money, but he felt it would bother him more to not explain the reality of the situation. It would almost be like lying, and he didn't want to lie. Not to her. "Well, I don't normally spend crazy amounts of money on things, but money isn't really an issue. My parents bought the ranch before I was born. A few years later, when I was a little kid, they found oil on the land. There's enough saved up to keep things going."

He hoped she didn't ask more questions, because he didn't want to have to say exactly how much money his family had.

"And you're still on the ranch? Why didn't you go

all *Beverly Hillbillies* and find someplace else to live in a city or something?"

"My parents bought the ranch because they wanted to live on a ranch, so the oil was just a bonus. They got a divorce and my dad moved to Houston when I was about seventeen. They sold the mineral rights to the oil so they could split everything, but my mom refused to give up the land. She loved the ranch and stayed there until she died six years ago. I came back from college to keep everything running smoothly."

"And you still live there. Is anybody else there with you?"

"No. I have a sister, but she moved to Washington, DC, for college and hasn't even considered coming back. My dad's still in Houston."

He didn't like dredging up the past, and hoped she wouldn't ask any more questions. His dad's infidelity, his parents' divorce and his mom's death were topics of conversation he avoided whenever possible. Her eyes held sympathy for him, which with most women would have annoyed him, but with her it was almost a little comforting.

"Do you want to talk about all this?"

"No."

He waited to see if he'd been too blunt, but she just nodded and stood up, piling their plates together. "Well, then, what should we do? We can go out on the town, watch a movie or whatever else comes to your mind."

"You realize I'm a guy and you're wearing nothing but a robe in my hotel room, right? Because if you're serious about doing something that comes to my mind, it could get graphic pretty fast."

He smiled at her to show he was teasing, but instead of laughing or rolling her eyes or any of the reactions he expected, she walked over to him and straddled him on the chair, her flowing robe leaving little to the imagination. She leaned in close to his ear, and in a velvety whisper said, "That's what I was hoping for."

Before he could react, she was up again and sweeping the dishes into the sink. He shook his head, trying to get his bearings back. How could she be so consistently astounding? He was instantly aroused, and she was standing in the kitchen as if nothing had happened. "You did that on purpose, didn't you?"

"Seemed like the thing to do," she responded airily.

He watched her as she tidied up. Though she didn't look at him, her lips turned up at the corners into a devious smile. She was probably very pleased with herself. He couldn't help smiling, too. *She might kill me before the weekend is over.*

He walked up behind her and slid his hand inside the robe's opening, sliding his palm across her stomach and lower to her hip, only inches from her core. He pressed himself against her, nipped lightly at her ear, and breathed, "I think we should—" He paused to suck lightly on her earlobe for a second, causing her to inhale sharply.

Then he moved away and turned toward the living area and finished with "—watch a movie."

He sat on the couch, barely able to keep from laughing as he turned on the TV. She came over to sit as close to him as possible, her hip pressed against his. He turned slightly toward her, and their eyes connected. He put his arm around her shoulders and pulled her toward him. She curled herself into his hold and shifted her legs off the floor so they were lying across his. She pressed her lips to his, and he held her closer.

For a moment, his mind flashed with regret that this would be gone from his life as quickly as it had entered, but then he focused once more on the kiss and shoved away that unpleasant thought.

Jessica pushed him down onto the couch, her legs straddling him, his erection pressed against her stomach as she leaned in and kissed him.

"This is a much better choice than a movie," he said against her lips, his voice rough and throaty.

"Much better," she agreed, and the deep whisper shot all the way through him, settling pleasantly in his groin.

She shifted herself higher, sliding along him and making him moan from the sensation, his head falling back onto the cushion as he tried to hold himself together. She was so sexy he could hardly believe it.

And then her weight was gone, leaving him alone on the couch. He sat up, disappointed, but only for a moment until he realized where she was going.

Jessica scurried over to the bed and went straight for the drawer where he'd placed a pack of condoms. He smiled at her as she came back to the couch at a near-run. "You seem a little impatient," he teased, ignoring how his cock jumped at the sight of her breasts bouncing with her movements.

She set the condom on the nearby coffee table. "Just want to have it nearby. For later," she explained.

Instead of resuming her place on top of him as he expected, however, she knelt on the floor beside the couch and slid her tongue along the length of him before taking him into her mouth.

The hot wetness of her tongue made him groan. *Whoa.* "That's not fair," he managed to get out between clenched teeth.

"What do you mean, 'not fair'?" she asked, her hot breath sending even more sensations rolling through him.

Instead of answering—which he wasn't sure he could even do at the moment—he lifted her back onto the couch in one quick motion and kissed her long and hard, enjoying the taste of her until she was panting.

Then, before she could get her bearings enough to continue with her relentless teasing, he slid one hand along her thigh, dipping into her wetness. She gasped, but he kept kissing her as he played with her, feeling her body react to his touch.

She pulled away just far enough to say, "Get the condom," and then she was kissing him again, her tongue sliding urgently into his mouth, demanding more.

He considered making her wait, but she was too goddamn sexy to do anything but obey. In seconds it was on and she was pushing him down on his back again, straddling him, her opening poised above him. "Ready, cowboy?"

She gave him no time to answer, even if he'd been able to. Without hesitation, she slid down him, enveloping him. He groaned her named as she moved on top of him, her movements fast, almost desperate.

She was in control, taking what she wanted, and he was loving every second of it. He looked up and watched her, her hair falling over her shoulders, her beautiful body on display just for him.

He didn't know what he'd do when they parted ways, but he was definitely enjoying the ride.

THE NEXT MORNING, Aaron relaxed on the bed and watched Jessica sleep. She was so beautiful sleeping, but he felt the urge to wake her up so he could see her green eyes looking into his, hear her talk about anything that came into her mind. He wanted to hear whatever she might say.

He hadn't realized how much he missed conversations like theirs from the night before, but if he was honest with himself, he'd had precious few of them since leaving college. He'd been starving for them without knowing it. For the past six years, he kept every thought about literature and world events pretty much to himself. Jeremiah and his other friends back home were great, but they didn't have any interest in those topics of discussion.

If he let himself think about it, he was dreading saying goodbye and going home. Now that he'd had so much, how could he be content with less? He didn't want to ruin his last full day with those kinds of thoughts, though, so he refocused his attention on her, memorizing her face and the way her hair spilled across the pillow.

She moved, stretching her long figure, and opened her eyes. She looked over and smiled at him. He smiled back. "Good morning, Jessica."

"Good morning. Last night was fun. Best movie I've seen in a long time."

He laughed. They'd gotten so distracted that they never actually made it through even a small part of a movie. He didn't think they'd even managed to turn one on. "Yeah, it was amazing."

They got up and put back on the robes from the night before, and set about ordering breakfast. Once that was done, Jessica began to pry once again into Aaron's plans for the day.

"I need to know what we're doing so I can go back to the room and get dressed. I only have jeans and a T-shirt."

"I helped you take off your jacket yesterday, remember? Definitely no shirt. I remember it vividly."

"It's in my purse. But if we're going somewhere, I'll need to get something to wear. So you have to tell me."

He shook his head. "Nope. I'm not going to tell you. You'll have to see for yourself. The things you have with you will be perfect."

"Are we going downtown? Someplace on the Strip? Those are the only places I know of here, so I'm out of guesses."

"It's neither of those. You're never going to be able to figure it out, so just relax. We'll leave in a couple hours. Until then, let's enjoy the morning."

She looked as if she was considering guessing some more, but she either thought better of it or couldn't think of anything, so instead she came over to the couch where he was sitting and curled herself onto his lap. "Fine, don't tell me."

He put his arms around her, pulling her warm body close to him, enjoying the weight of her on his legs and chest. "You'll find out soon enough. It's not some giant amazing surprise or anything. It's just hard to explain."

"Okay, just get me back by five or so. I've got to spend time with Cindy or she'll kill me."

"Deal." He kissed her forehead and rested his head against hers.

He knew he was getting himself in way too deep with her, but he didn't want to stop. As he sat there holding her, he decided that he was going to get every-thing he could out of that day, even if it meant a little misery later on. He'd just have to get over it. There was no point trying to keep his distance and missing out on this amazing moment in his life.

He was absolutely addicted to her. Her eyes, her hair, her smell, her body, her brain were all mind-blowingly fantastic, and he was never going to see her again? That made no sense.

When the food arrived and Jessica uncurled herself and padded to the door on bare feet, he watched her. He didn't want to let her disappear out of his life com-pletely. He needed to find a way to make it work, and before she got on her plane, he was going to have some assurance that he'd see her again.

With that positive thought, he hopped up and helped her, and soon they were eating at the table. After, they enjoyed another long shower together. He loved running his soapy hands along her smooth skin, down her back and along the sides of her stomach to her ticklish spot that made her wriggle away. Every inch was magnificent.

When they were finally rinsed and dried and dressed, he called the driver and arranged for them to be picked up at the front of the hotel. He grabbed his coat out of the closet and draped it over his arm. "It's good you brought your jacket. It could get cold out there."

He could see her mind using this clue to try to figure out exactly where they were going. "Dammit, I don't know this area well enough. Are you going to take me out in the middle of the desert? Because that's what serial killers and mobster hit men do."

"You must have been such an obnoxious kid around Christmastime. Did you ever make it to the twenty-fifth without guessing every present?"

"Oh, I was the worst. It drove my parents crazy. We had to have all sorts of rules about not touching the presents, and they never answered any of my questions. My dad—"

She stopped talking and looked embarrassed for a moment. He almost asked what was wrong, but she looked as if she didn't want to talk about it, and he decided not to push for details.

They left the room and made it down the elevator, through the casino and into the car before she said anything more, but she didn't act as though she was upset or anything. Just quiet. He noted that she chose to sit in the middle seat, despite the large empty area available to her, and his stomach warmed. She wanted to sit closer to him. As he sat beside her and buckled his seat belt, she turned back to the topic of the surprise. "So, not the middle of the desert, right?"

"No, we're not going to the middle of a barren waste-land where people bury dead bodies. Satisfied?"

"Well, at least then I would've known where we're going. Okay, I'll wait. How long until we get there? How are you going to let the driver know where to take us if it's such a secret?"

"He already knows, and about forty minutes. No more questions, okay?"

She nodded and sat back, seemingly content. "Right. No more questions. I'm going to sit back and relax. I'll just text Cindy to let her know that I'll be at dinner."

It took him about fifteen seconds to realize she wasn't texting and leaned over to see a map of Las Vegas on her phone. "Oh my God. Seriously, you have a problem."

He snagged the phone out of her hand and held it away from her, amused at her complete refusal to be surprised. When she tried to grab it back, he tucked it underneath himself and caught her up in his arms, pressing his mouth against hers to distract her.

She stopped struggling for the phone and allowed him to hold her close, and the kiss soon became hungry and urgent. By the time they split apart, both were panting and he wished they were back in his room. They leaned away from each other without breaking eye contact, taking in deep breaths to regain composure.

Once he had calmed himself enough, he pulled the phone out from under him and said, "We've built this surprise thing up way too much, and you're going to be disappointed now. I'm just taking you to a place that's near Vegas and happens to be kind of cool. You can keep searching if you want."

He passed the small device over to her, and she glanced at it for a moment before throwing it back in her purse. "If you're not going to try to stop me, what's the fun in that? Let me know when we get there."

With that, she closed her eyes and leaned against him. He wrapped his arm around her, and she settled deeper into the nook, her head against his shoulder. He could tell when she fell asleep, her breathing slow and deep, and he felt contentedness seeping through him.

Neither of them had gotten much sleep the past couple of nights, but instead of allowing himself to nod off as well, he spent the rest of the trip enjoying the feeling of her body against his, his mind quiet except for the question of how to get her to agree to see him again, which simmered lightly in the back of his brain.

One of the first steps, he realized, was to let Olivia know he wasn't interested anymore. If he was going to be worthy of Jessica, he couldn't leave that tie unsevered. He pulled his phone out of his pocket with his one free hand, careful not to move much, letting her sleep. He turned it on with a swipe, considering his options.

He couldn't just say it over a text, though. That was cowardly, and besides, she probably wouldn't get the hint, if the last time he talked to her was any indication. He'd have to talk to her in person. Finally he settled on meeting her when Jessica was with her friends. That way, he wouldn't have to waste any of his last few hours with Jessica on anything but being with her.

He composed the text carefully, trying to be polite but distant. It took some time to decide exactly what to say and then type it one-handed, but he finally sent, Hey, Olivia, if you have time this evening, I'd like to meet up and talk for a few minutes. Are you free at all between seven and nine tonight? You don't have to worry about coming over. I'll drive wherever.

He was sure he could have come up with something better, but under the circumstances he hoped it would be enough to give her a small clue so their conversation wouldn't be a total shock. He put his phone back in his pocket and looked out the window.

The city was behind them, and the car swept along a nearly empty highway surrounded by desert and dark, barren mountains. He didn't know why he thought it was so beautiful. Most people would see it as some scrub brush and a few sad mountains devoid of trees, but the power of the desert and the number of plants that managed to still live in it had always impressed him. Except for the small pockets of a few run-down houses, nature was still in control.

When they were close to their destination, he shifted himself slightly, using his free hand to brush the hair out of Jessica's face. He half whispered, "Jessica, we're almost there."

Her eyes fluttered open and she sat up with a yawn and looked at the desert spread out around them. "I never thought the desert would be beautiful. Now that

I see it up close, there's something about it that makes my soul jump. Did that make any sense at all?"

She looked at him for confirmation. "I love it," he answered. "I can't explain why, either. Every time I come to Vegas, I get out of the city for at least a few hours. There's a big mountain out here that's got some cool hiking trails, but I wasn't sure you'd like that and it's pretty cold. I think they've already opened the ski lifts."

"There are ski lifts in Las Vegas?" she responded, surprised.

He nodded. "Yeah, but I wasn't sure that would be fun for you, so we're in the Valley of Fire. It's named that because of all the red stone around here."

He gestured out his window, drawing her attention toward the rock formations. He continued. "We can go out for a little bit and walk around. There's one rock formation that looks like an elephant and stuff like that. As soon as you want to leave, though, we can head back."

Before he'd finished, she was wiggling herself into her jacket and unbuckling her seat belt. "Let's go! I haven't climbed around on rocks since I was a kid. Not many opportunities in New York."

He inhaled deeply as they left the car. The air was cool and fresh, and the desert stretched around them, vast and unforgiving. Vegas was a faint squiggle in the distance. Aaron loved getting away from the city and onto the land, and it seemed Jessica felt the same way despite living in one of the biggest cities in the world.

She turned full circle to take it all in, sun glinting in her hair and turning it a thousand shades of red and gold. Once she made her circuit and was facing him again, she grinned, her sparkling green eyes grabbing at him, pulling him in. "This is perfect."

His heart hit so hard against his ribs he wanted to rub the spot. "Perfect," he agreed.

But he wasn't thinking about their surroundings.

They stared at each other for a long second, and the couple of feet of air between them felt absurd. Aaron wanted to pull her in to him, wrap his fingers in her hair, but they were so far from the hotel and their driver was sitting in the car less than twenty feet away. And he wanted her to experience this place.

Reluctantly he shifted and pointed up a small thin trail. She turned to face the direction he pointed, and the moment was gone. He would hold her close later, he promised himself. There would be other moments.

Not as many as he wanted, though. It hurt just thinking about getting on a plane and flying away from her.

He shoved the thought to the back of his mind and tried to focus on the here and now. "Up that way about a mile is the elephant. You want to see it?"

She started toward the trail in response, and he fell in step beside her. They walked quietly for a short time, and his mind wandered back to the airplane. Truth was, he wanted to see her again. Maybe even needed to see her again. This couldn't be it. But if she said no again?

He opened his mouth to bring up the subject, but before he could say anything, she pointed to a large boulder ahead and asked, "See that rock?"

Nothing seemed particularly special about it. Just a big red rock. "Yeah."

With that, she took off running, shouting, "Race you!" as she went.

He was so surprised it took him a second to realize what was happening. By the time he started running, she had a huge lead, and even though he ran as fast as he could, faster than he'd run since he was a kid, she still managed to beat him by a couple of yards.

She leaned against the rock, her arms crossed, her grin triumphant. He tried to look disapproving, but it was impossible not to smile. "You cheated. That absolutely doesn't count."

She only held her chin higher. "Sorry, what did you say? It's hard to hear you over all the winning."

He had to laugh. "Fine. Congratulations on winning by cheating. Cheater."

She smiled, apparently satisfied with his remark. God, he liked her. When was the last time he'd just had fun like this? Even counting time with Jeremiah, it had been years.

He pointed to another rock. "How about we do that again, but fair this time? I'll race you to that one on the count of three."

She shrugged and started sauntering down the path. "No, I don't feel like it right now."

He walked at her side, eyeing her. As he suspected, she bolted after a few steps. He was prepared this time and caught up almost instantly, beating her to the finish line with time to spare. He leaned against the rock, mimicking her pose from before. As she stopped beside him, he shook his head. "Even with you cheating, *again*, I won. What do you have to say about that, Miss 'Let's race'?"

Her expression was almost neutral, but the tilt to the corner of her lips and the brightness of her eyes made it clear she was holding back laughter. "Well, of course you beat me! You're a guy. And you run. I'm a proper lazy American."

Something about what she said struck him as odd. "Wait, I run? How do you know I run?"

She blushed a little, and it reminded him of the way her skin flushed as he touched her. He felt his own temperature rise.

She waved her hand in the vague direction of Las Vegas. "On Friday, I was standing outside the Venetian and you ran by."

She was trying to say it as though it were a minor, throwaway event, but her flush told him it was more. He smiled and nodded. "Liked what you saw, huh?"

She rolled her eyes, but the red in her cheeks darkened. He couldn't hold himself back any longer. In one lithe movement, he reached over and grabbed her hand, pulling her in toward him.

She fell into his arms and his lips planted onto hers. She seemed surprised for only a moment before pressing in against him, pushing him into the rock behind him. One of his hands wound into her hair, and the other curled around her waist, sliding down over her bottom.

Aaron was grateful for the privacy of the rocks that surrounded them. Then Jessica's tongue slid across his teeth and all thinking stopped as desire mushroomed through him. In a manner of seconds she was pressed against the rock and he was on top of her, his fingers under blouse, teasing at her nipple through the fabric of her bra. He could feel the hard nub of it, and her breath became ragged against his mouth. One hand reached toward the buttons of her jeans.

And then she started chuckling. His fingers stopped the exploration and he leaned back a little. Her eyes were closed, her skin flushed, and she let her head fall against the rock. His mind finally caught up, realizing where they were and what they were doing.

She sighed, smiling at him, her eyes still closed. "This is the greatest weekend ever."

He laughed and leaned next to her. "Yeah, it is. Should we go see the elephant thing?"

She nodded, but her look of disappointment sent a little wave of happiness through him. Her passionate side blew his mind. Brushing his lips against her shoulder, he said, "We can continue this back at the hotel after."

She seemed pleased at the idea. As she began to move away from the rock, setting herself to rights and walking toward the trail, he grabbed her hand, interlacing his fingers with hers. "Now you can't cheat at any more races," he explained.

It was probably obvious to her that he just wanted to keep touching her, but he didn't care.

The next couple of hours flew by as they explored the area. Aaron loved how willing Jessica was to climb over anything, try any challenge. He couldn't believe she was so excited to be there, and every passing minute he liked her more and more, which he'd been sure was impossible just a few hours ago. There were a few more kisses against the rocks, but he was able to keep himself in control. Mostly.

By the time they clambered back into the waiting car, her cheeks and nose were red from the cool air, her hair was a mess, her clothes were dusty and she was wearing a huge, cheerful grin. He loved how her eyes glittered when she was happy, and she was happy because of him. All she said, though, was a quiet "Good surprise" as she rested herself against him.

He leaned his cheek against her forehead. *Maybe she's just enjoying a fun weekend*, he thought, *but maybe this is more for her, too.*

He knew that he'd have to talk to her about it before the next morning. But not yet. If he had misread things, he didn't want to ruin this moment.

So instead he just enjoyed the drive.

10

SHE LEANED AGAINST HIM, happy and exhausted, but inside she felt a hint of fear. This was going too far, and she felt powerless to stop herself. She'd almost told him about her father, which was just insane. Why would she share the most difficult part of her life with a near stranger?

He didn't feel like a stranger, though. A big part of her regretted that she hadn't agreed to see him again. Her feelings had gotten out of her control. She liked him far more than was good for her.

She'd even started hoping that he would ask again. She didn't know what her answer would be. The more she thought about it, the more muddled she felt, so instead she just relaxed against his side and engulfed herself in his warmth and his smell. Big decisions could wait until the next day.

He wrapped his arm tighter around her, squeezing her slightly. He said, "Oh, hey. I got some playing cards down at the gift shop on my way back from the rodeo yesterday. Forgot to mention it. We have enough time when we get back for me to destroy you at poker before you need to leave."

He really would destroy her at poker, but she found the idea amusing rather than intimidating. It was weird to think that he was the only man she had ever dated whom she didn't mind losing to. *No. Not dating. Just a Vegas fling*, she reminded herself sternly with a small shake of her head. Thinking of this thing as a date was dangerous. *Screw you, Cody-the-dealer, and your love talk.*

She pushed the thought away. "Sounds fun. Do you have poker chips?"

His mouth turned up into the crooked smile she liked so much. "Nope. We'll have to play strip poker or something."

The idea sent a thrill through her.

When they arrived back at his hotel room, they were both quiet and relaxed. She still had a couple of hours before she had to leave to get ready for dinner with Cindy—plenty of time for anything. Aaron looked at her with an eyebrow raised. "Robes?"

"I thought we were going to play strip poker?"

His grin told her everything she wanted to know.

"Robes," she agreed.

Soon they were both clad only in the soft fluffiness of the Hard Rock's luxury robes. He went to the bathroom while she relaxed on the couch, waiting for him to come back, the expectation of their afternoon charging the air around her.

A phone on the table beside her vibrated and lit up. She glanced at it automatically before realizing her phone was still in her purse. Before the screen went dark, she saw the name of the person who had texted Aaron, and felt pulled to turn on the screen and read the text that had shown up below the name Olivia.

Before she could stop herself, her finger pressed the home button and the phone lit up. The entire text showed on the lock screen, and before it turned dark again, she'd read the entire message. Olivia had written Seven works for me. I'll talk to you tonight!

He was meeting another girl as soon as she left for dinner. Jessica's stomach twisted and she found it hard to breathe. She leaned back, away from the phone, and inhaled slowly and deeply. Why had she expected anything different? She'd seen him outside the strip club. She knew that was the kind of guy he was.

In fact, she decided, she wasn't sad about the situation, just mad that she had let herself think anything other than what her rational mind had been telling her all along. She knew he'd been with plenty of women. That was the main reason she'd decided never to see him again. Still, she had been hoping that maybe he'd be able to change, to settle down and stick to just one woman. Despite her head's intention to leave everything in Vegas, her heart had been hoping they could somehow find a way to be together.

That was stupid. She saw that clearly. Nothing had changed between her and Aaron, because this was the expectation all along. It was a fun weekend thing, and she should've known that he would find something to do while she was gone. And that something's name was Olivia.

Despite everything she told herself, though, all the logical reasons why she shouldn't feel upset, she wanted nothing more than to run out the door. The walls of the giant room felt far too close and she longed to be anywhere else, but she worked to get herself tightly under control. Aaron was going to return any moment, and she had to get back to normal before he did.

Since it was very clear from the outset that they weren't going to be some long-term exclusive couple, she couldn't fault him for her emotions getting away from her. She just needed to keep things light and relaxed, which was exactly what she should've been doing all along.

When she heard the bathroom door open, she grabbed the TV remote. She didn't want to look guilty. With one last long, calming breath, Jessica turned on whatever movie the icon was on when the screen lit up. She didn't know what it was she turned on, but anything would be better than silence or something as intimate as the type of poker game he had suggested.

He came back into the room and sat down next to her, dropping his hand onto her thigh. "You'd rather watch a movie than play poker? What are we watching?"

Her throat felt tight and she didn't know if she wanted to slap his hand away or curl herself up against him. She chose to stay still and forced her voice to come out even. "I'm not sure. I just turned on whatever."

He glanced at her, then looked again more closely, and she knew she was doing a terrible job of letting go of what she'd seen. She wanted to leave things on good terms, but she had to get out of there. His look of concern grew more pronounced as she stood up. "Hey, is everything okay?"

She tried to make her voice as light as possible. "Yes, I just realized that I really should get back and get ready for that dinner thing. I can't sit around here the whole day."

She grabbed her clothes as quickly as possible and walked into the bedroom, forcing herself not to lock the door. She reminded herself again that he hadn't done anything wrong and didn't deserve to be given a cold shoulder from her.

She was dressed in a flash and back out into the living room. He was still sitting on the couch, but his whole body was turned toward her, and his face showed absolute perplexity. "What's wrong? What's going on? Did something happen?"

She brushed his questions aside with a wave of her hand. "Nothing's wrong. It's just me. I have to deal with some things, but it has nothing to do with you."

She walked over quickly to give him a peck on the cheek to show him and herself that everything was fine, but he turned his head as she kissed him, pressing his lips hard against hers, his hand moving to the back of her head. She almost let herself fall into the kiss, and the wall she'd been rebuilding around her heart crumbled a little before she realized what was happening and pulled away. As she stood back up, he whispered, "Please don't go."

It tore at her, but she pretended she hadn't heard and turned toward the door. In the same light voice as before, she said, "Today was fun. I'm sorry I have to go, but enjoy your evening. I'll talk to you later."

Before he could say anything else or ask if she'd be coming back that night, she was out the door. She didn't want to have to answer questions. The elevator opened the moment she touched the button. As the doors slid shut behind her, she wasn't sure if she was relieved or disappointed that he hadn't come after her.

Her hand brushed away a few stray tears that had appeared on her cheeks. There was no reason to cry. She'd had an amazing weekend fling with an attractive cowboy, and now it was over. Time to get back to her real life and stop the fantasy nonsense. Fantasies don't work well in real life.

By the time the elevator stopped at the casino level, she was under control. She strode through the banks of slot machines and out the door into the bright sunlight. Taxis were lined up waiting for customers, and one whisked her away to her own hotel.

Sitting in the back, she told herself once again that, really, she was making the right choice, not seeing him again. She didn't want a guy in her life, even if he did have eyes that made her blood run hot and hands that made her tremble with pleasure. Even if his smile melted her inside and he was funny and smart.

She brought her legs up onto the seat and wrapped her arms around them, holding her body together with all her strength. At the hotel, she paid the fare and walked upstairs quietly and with all the serenity she could muster. Once she was alone in the hotel room, though, the tears came hot and fast, and she let them.

After a while, she pulled herself back together and began dressing for dinner. She wasn't sure what level of attire was appropriate, but neither did she care much. Once her hair was tied in a bun and she was in whatever outfit was nearest, she headed to Cindy's room.

The moment Cindy opened the door, her expression immediately transformed into one of shock. "Oh my God, what did the bastard do? Are you okay?"

Jessica was taken aback. "What do you mean? I'm fine."

Cindy scoffed. "No, you're not. I know what you normally look like. This red-eyed girl with the hang-dog expression is not you. You look worse than when you came over after the Russ incident."

Apparently her efforts to pull things together were not completely successful. "I'm fine. I've decided not to see Aaron again. I let myself get too close, and started to forget that it was just a weekend fling, but it's fine. Don't worry, really. We're going back to New York tomorrow and I'll only remember it as a fun Vegas thing. It'll be fine."

"You said fine way too many times. Did you try to set up something so you'd see each other again? Did he say he only wanted a weekend fling? Was that it?"

Jessica chuckled lightly, but there was no humor in the effort. "Actually he asked me if he could come to New York sometime, but I turned him down. And it was a good choice. He just wants another woman on the side that he can sleep with when he's in town and forget the minute he leaves. I don't want to be that woman, so—"

"Hold up. I'm confused. Start the story from the beginning. I'll text the girls we'll have dinner in an hour or so and we'll get this figured out."

Despite Jessica's protest, Cindy sent the text and sat down, crossing her arms, to hear the story.

Jessica sighed and sat beside her. She went through everything that had happened that day, from their conversation in bed to the trip out of town to the text message she saw.

She concluded, "It isn't because he's seeing someone else tonight—he has all the right in the world to do that when we're just having fun—my emotions about the situation made it very clear that I shouldn't get any closer. So I left."

She expected sympathy from Cindy, but she didn't get it. "Why didn't you ask him about the text? It specifically said the word *talk* in it, right? How do you know he was planning on anything other than talking to her?"

Jessica was aghast. "You think he was just going to get coffee or something with some old female friend and I misunderstood the situation? Are you kidding?"

Cindy's expression softened. "I think that Russ hurt you and you've been so closed off from people for so long that you can't trust others anymore, and that's sad. You used to be warm and open, but for the past two months you haven't let anyone get close to you. I think this guy was finally brushing away some of that and helping you get back to the old you. And I think he must either really like you or be the biggest womanizer on the planet if half the things you said are true. Why not ask and find out?"

Jessica put her face in her hands. "I can't do that."

"I know what it's like to be hurt. Everyone does. But that doesn't mean you don't get a chance at real love. Look at me."

Jessica looked over her fingers and saw Cindy's small smile as she looked at her engagement ring. Her heart took on a life of its own, twisting and writhing in envy. She wanted that.

In the silence, her phone went off, loud and shrill. For a moment, she was sure it was Aaron calling, despite the fact that she had never given him her number. Then she looked and saw it was her sister, Renee.

That was an odd occurrence. Renee never called, preferring to text any conversations. She answered, perplexed and momentarily distracted. "Hey, Renee."

"Jessica—"

She could hear the tears in her sister's voice, and her throat tightened in panic. "Renee, what is it? What's going on?"

The voice that responded trembled with barely subdued emotion. "Dad's back in the hospital."

Jessica felt her body go cold. She'd known it could happen anytime, but it still seemed unreal. "How bad is it?" she whispered, her voice breaking.

"Bad. You need to get here. Now."

That wasn't what she wanted to hear, but she'd known it was coming. This wasn't a time to cry or panic, though. She stood, mentally listing what she would need to do to get out of Vegas as soon as possible. She said, "I'm on my way," and hung up before her sister could respond.

Cindy was looking at her with concern. Jessica

started toward the door. "I have to go back home. It's my dad."

Cindy nodded. "I'll look up flights. I won't be able to book anything for you, but at least you'll know how much time you have to pack and get to the airport."

Jessica hugged her friend before half running to her hotel room. Within five minutes, her belongings were packed and she was in her travel clothes, ready for the flight. As she packed the last of her things, there was a knock on the door. She hoped with all her heart it would be Aaron. They might not have time to talk, but she could at least give him her phone number.

It wasn't him on the other side of the door, though. Cindy was there with flight information written down. If she hurried, she'd just be able to make the flight leaving in a little over an hour. The next one would get her home over five hours later.

She bolted to the elevators and pressed the button frantically. "Cindy, I'm so sorry for everything this weekend. Tell the other girls I'm sorry, too. I really did enjoy getting to know them a little bit. I'll make it up to you."

Cindy shrugged and gave her a watery smile that seemed close to tears. "Don't worry about it. Just get home to your family. Do you want me to do anything about Aaron?"

The elevator dinged and opened as Jessica grasped her friend into one last tight hug and took the sheet with the flight details; she walked on, rolling her small suitcase behind her. "If you can find him, tell him what happened and give him my phone number. We need to talk."

Once she got to the lobby, she practically flew to the taxi stand, and was immediately ushered into a waiting cab. She asked him to take her to the airport as quickly as he could, then called the number Cindy had written. By the time the taxi pulled up to the airport, she was scheduled for the flight and had her boarding pass loaded on her phone.

She only had thirty-two minutes to make it through the airport, but she was not going to miss that flight. A hurried conversation with a TSA agent and she was bypassing the line at security. Rushing through, she was on the other side in record-breaking time. Her shoes were in her hands when she saw the tram that would take her to the right terminal arrive, so she held on to them and ran over in her socks. She managed to board a moment before the doors closed with a snap.

On the tram, she took a moment to breathe and put on her shoes. It was too much to think about her family, about her father who had always been there for her, so instead she thought of Aaron. Not how she walked out with him looking at her, but instead of his smile as he said that he wanted to see her again, and the light in his eyes as they ran around out in the desert.

Cindy would find him, she assured herself. She'd texted her friend his hotel information, and she trusted Cindy to do what she'd promised. She was a good friend to have around in a crisis.

The tram stopped after what seemed far too long of a

ride, and Jessica was the first one out, rushing through the airport to her gate, which of course had to be the one farthest away. When she reached the door, they were making the last call for passengers. Her ticket was scanned and she was rushing down the gangplank before she could pause for breath.

Once she stepped on the plane and was moving slowly through the crush of seats and passengers, she tried to take calming breaths. Her heart was pounding so hard it hurt, from both the dash to the plane and the stress of the situation. She tried to tell herself that whatever happened, she was on her way home and that was the best she could do.

It didn't help much.

Finding her seat, she strapped herself in. She sent a few last messages to her mother and sister, one last message to Cindy thanking her and then she put her phone in airplane mode and leaned back in her seat, still gasping. So much had happened that she couldn't wrap her mind around it all, and the whir of thoughts made her almost nauseated.

She pulled out her headphones and set her playlist to The Beatles and the volume as loud as she could stand. She rarely listened to music, usually preferring audiobooks, but she knew that anything involving focus would be a lost cause; her goal was to drown out her thoughts as much as possible.

She leaned against the window and somehow, miraculously, she slept.

AARON HURRIED THROUGH the airport looking for the right gate. The plane hadn't left yet, but it would be taking off any minute. When he saw it ahead, the area was deserted except for a flight attendant, and she rushed him through onto the plane.

Relieved he had made it in time, he hustled onto the plane, put his luggage in the overhead compartment and looked around. The flight wasn't very full, which was a bit surprising. After a cursory glance, he sat in his seat and buckled his seat belt. In just over three hours he'd be back in Texas, but that was not soon enough. The faster he could get the hell out of Vegas, the better.

He felt angry at nobody in particular, and wanted nothing but to be left alone. He still couldn't believe what had happened. Jessica had run out that afternoon because of a stupid misunderstanding that was completely his fault.

Once he saw Olivia's text a few minutes after Jessica had taken off, he realized exactly what must have happened, what she thought. He didn't blame her for her reaction. After he'd heard what had happened with her last boyfriend, it made perfect sense, and it killed him that he had caused her that kind of pain.

He decided to give her a little time before rushing over. If she was mad, he wanted her to be at least calm enough to listen to him. He spent that time on the phone with Olivia breaking things off for good—he felt like an ass doing it over the phone, but he couldn't bring himself to go over and see her when things were so confused. After he felt enough time had passed, he'd gone over to Jessica's hotel and up to her room, only to find nobody there.

Without her phone number, there was nothing he could do but go down to the casino and look for the group of women in the nearest restaurants, hoping they were having dinner somewhere nearby. He wandered around for nearly an hour before going back up to her room, determined to sit outside the door and wait for her.

He had been frustrated by that point, but not at her. He was mad at himself for not talking to her the moment he'd realized he wanted to be more than just an occasional fling.

Sitting on the plane headed back home, he still wasn't sure what he would've said if she had shown up. He had only known that he couldn't let her disappear out of his life for good. So he had sat there until a woman walked by who looked vaguely familiar. She stopped and looked him up and down slowly. She seemed to like what she saw, because her voice came out as a purr.

"Hey, sweetie. Can I help you with something?"

He didn't want to be rude, but by that time he was tired and had been looking for so long that his patience had run short. He tilted his head toward the door, his facial expression flat. "I'm here for Jessica."

"Jessica left a while ago. She had to fly back home. Family trouble."

With that, he'd been done with Vegas. He felt frustrated that he'd lost his chance to explain, guilty that he had hurt her even inadvertently and appalled that he would never see her again. He considered trying to get her number from the woman but realized that if he'd hurt her enough to make up a reason to leave Vegas early just to get away from him, she probably didn't want to hear from him, even if he was going to explain.

She probably wouldn't even believe him. Her history would make it hard to trust anyone, and that included the guy who she very definitely thought was only interested in no-strings-attached flings. She had a point there, after all. That was the way he'd been for years, and she had spotted it almost immediately. It was too much to expect her to believe in a sudden change of heart.

After his unsuccessful stakeout, he had gone back to his hotel, grabbed his things and headed to the airport. He changed his flight and was glad to watch the lights of Vegas disappear into the distance. He knew things wouldn't be exactly the same once he got to Texas. After all, he couldn't go back in time or erase her from his memory.

Still, at least he'd be home.

11

JESSICA WOKE UP just as the plane was starting its descent. She felt a little better, a little more clearheaded, despite her anxiety about her father. She hadn't gotten much information from her sister, and all she could do was hope she would be back in time. The light of the sunrise streaming through the window told her it would be early morning when they touched down. She had been so busy rushing to change her flight and get on it that she hadn't considered what time it would land, but she should have expected the evening flight cross-country and the time change to find her arriving the next day.

The moment the plane landed, her phone was out of airplane mode and she was sending and receiving messages.

Renee responded, He's alive and awake. Get here when you can.

Jessica wiped the few tears from her face. It was very clear, though her sister never said it, that he wouldn't be around much longer. Even though she'd been prepared for this circumstance for almost a year, it didn't erase the pain. Her dad was dying and there was nothing she could do but be there holding his hand when he went.

There was also a message from Cindy. Hey, Jess. Went to his room, knocked on the door. Waited, but he didn't show. I'm so sorry. I'll try again before the flight. Love you.

Jessica didn't think she had any emotion left to spare for Aaron with everything going on, but she still felt a stab of pain. There were few good reasons she could think of that would explain his absence, and the possibility seemed much more real that she would, in fact, never see him again.

She couldn't let herself think about all that. She had enough to deal with already. She left the plane and headed toward the taxis. Normally she would take the subway, but speed was the issue, not expense. Once she was in the vehicle and they were on the way to the hospital, she allowed herself to consider the situation. Her father had been slowly losing his battle for a long time, and though he had been positive and put forth the effort to make things seem less dire, they had known this day was coming.

A small secret part of her knew it was for the best for them all. He had been in so much pain that her mom's entire life had been put on hold, and she and her sister had avoided doing anything too big, too far away, so that they could be around at a moment's notice. It was hard to admit, but they'd all needed this moment to arrive.

It didn't stop it from hurting, though. Her heart felt as if it had been through a wringer during the past twenty-four hours, and she wished there was a way to numb the pain a little. If she had someone to hold her and comfort her, strong arms keeping her close…

Just a few hours ago, she would have tried to stop the fantasy, to avoid the possibility that she would let herself fall into a trap, but now she allowed herself to take comfort in the picture. She mentally curled herself into the crook of his arm, feeling his warmth.

The taxi pulled up to the hospital, and she strode in, directing her steps straight toward the elevator and the room her sister had sent her. She walked steadily, but her mind felt as if it were floating above her body, and the whole situation lacked the feeling of reality.

In the elevator, she took a few deep breaths to try to bring herself back together. It was important to be calm when she saw her family, but it was much more important that she be all *there*. She didn't want to ever look back at this time and think she'd glazed over it. It had to stay true to life, no matter how painful.

She walked into the hospital room, and there he was. Her father, obscured somewhat by tubes and other medical devices, looked so much smaller than she pictured him, even though she'd only seen him a few days before.

Renee and her mom moved from their positions at the bedside to hug her. Neither was crying, but their eyes were red and their faces were drawn. It was clear they'd had a rough time. Jessica was sure she didn't look much better.

Her mom whispered, "The doctors were in here just a little while ago. He's fading fast, but we've got some time still. They're not sure how much longer he'll be aware enough to know what's happening around him. They wanted to give him morphine for the pain, but he didn't want to take it until after you got back."

The tears glittered in her mother's eyes, and Jessica felt a few spill down her own cheeks. She nodded and gave a watery smile. Of course he said that. She would never have forgiven herself if she'd been too late, and he knew that. Family had always been her dad's number-one priority, and even now he was determined to do what he could to make things better for her.

She walked up to the bed and carefully held the frail hand in both of hers. The year before, he'd been a big, strong man who dwarfed most people. Since then, though, he'd slowly shrunk and shriveled, until she was afraid to squeeze him too tightly. His thick black hair had become light and wispy, and he looked far older than he should have. The change had been hard to watch, but he was still her dad through and through.

He opened his eyes and looked at her, and she saw the corners crinkle as he smiled at her. She smiled back, but her eyes filled with more tears. She was determined not to shed them in front of him, though. The room was quiet except for the machinery working to monitor his status and keep him alive. She spoke softly to him. "Hey, Dad. I'm here."

His voice was barely a whisper, so she leaned in close to hear him. "Hey, baby. I missed you. Did you have fun?"

She chuckled and shook her head. It was possibly the last time they'd ever speak, and he wanted to make sure she had a good time on her vacation. "Yeah, I had fun. Missed you, though."

"Sorry you had to cut it short."

"Vegas was too crazy for me, anyway."

He squinted slightly at her. "You look different. Good different."

She rolled her eyes. "Dad, I'm a mess. I've gotten almost no sleep for three days."

"Not that. Something happened. You look...sparkly."

His voice was so quiet that she wasn't sure she heard him correctly. "I look sparkly?"

He nodded, his head moving a fraction of an inch up and down. "It suits you. What happened?"

She'd always been able to tell her dad pretty much anything, but she didn't know how to explain the events from the weekend, and there wasn't much time left. "I met a guy. He was nice, but it got complicated. I don't know if I'll see him again."

The earnest look in his eyes made her heart clench. "You should. It's nice to see you happy."

She sank down into the chair by the bed, not moving her hands from his. Happiness was definitely not one of the emotions she was feeling, but she knew what he meant. "Thanks, Dad."

He nodded again and closed his eyes. "Love you, baby."

"Love you, too, Daddy."

She hoped he understood everything she meant when she said it. She lightly squeezed his hand and rested her forehead on the edge of the bed. She allowed herself to weep silently now that he couldn't see her.

She cried because he wouldn't be with her to give her advice anymore, because of how unfair it all was and because all she wanted to do was curl up in someone's arms, but she was alone.

She heard her father say her name quietly, and she quickly pulled herself together as much as she could. "What is it, Dad?"

"You'll be okay, Jessie. I'm not worried about you."

She closed her eyes and took a shuddering breath, nodding. "Thanks."

"Call the doctor. I'll take the medicine now."

Her mother and sister, who had been standing quietly in the corner of the room moved forward, and the three women huddled together next to his bed. Jessica pressed the call button, and they all three held his hand, waiting silently. He looked each of them in the eye, and his fingers pressed the lightest of squeezes against theirs. He whispered, "I love you so much," and a single tear slipped down his cheek.

Then he closed his eyes and relaxed his hold. The nurse entered, but none of them looked away from the figure on the bed. Jessica's mom, her voice calm and firm, said, "You can give him the morphine now."

THEY STAYED AT the hospital for two more days, but her dad never regained consciousness. Before he died, Jessica, her mother and her sister each took a few minutes alone to talk to him, despite knowing that he couldn't hear or respond.

When it was Jessica's turn, she sat down and held his hand once more. "Hi, Dad."

She looked at his face. He seemed so peaceful. "I just want you to know I love you. I don't really know what else to say. You've done so much to make my life wonderful. Thank you for everything. I'm going to try to make you proud of me."

She could practically hear his response to that, and she laughed lightly. "I know you'd say that you're proud of me no matter what, but you know what I mean. You've been telling me these past few months not to let what happened with Russ and your illness affect me, and I finally see what you mean. I didn't realize I'd been so scared to let anybody get close. I knew I had a wall around my heart, but I couldn't see how it was hurting me. I'm going to take more risks and keep my heart open, and even if I get hurt again, I'll be okay."

She paused for a moment to wipe away a few tears. "You remember that guy I met in Vegas? Cindy tried to find him for me, but I was too late. I waited too long to tell him what I wanted, to try something risky, and by the time I started to figure it out, he was gone. I waited and I lost. I'm not going to make a mistake like that again, Dad. I won't put that wall back up, and even if I can't find Aaron, I won't stop being sparkly, I promise."

She was crying openly now, but she did nothing to stop the flood as she finished. "I love you, Dad."

She pressed her face into the bedcovers and wept freely. After a few moments, she looked up, startled. She wasn't sure if she'd imagined it or it had actually happened, but she'd felt pressure on her hand, as if her dad had squeezed it. Jessica smiled at her father. Whether or not it really occurred didn't matter.

When he passed away a few hours later, Jessica stood with her sister and mother, holding them close.

The drive to her mother's home was quiet. It was midday, cold and sunny, but Jessica hardly registered the weather. There were too many things to think about. Her parents, always practical, had created a plan for this situation as soon as her father was diagnosed. Now that he was gone, the house would be going up for sale and her mother would be moving to an apartment near work and her friends.

They'd only owned the house a couple of years, so Jessica wasn't torn apart at the prospect of selling it, but she worried for her mother. Jessica looked at the older woman as they trudged in the door. She seemed tired, weighed down. The moment she was in the house, however, she went to the living room and began placing the last few pieces of memorabilia in a box that had been sitting in the corner of the room for months.

"Mom, you should take some time to rest," Jessica said.

Her mom, ever the one for proper etiquette, snorted. "That's a terrible idea. All the books say to deal with grief by keeping busy and having plans. That's what I'm doing."

However much her mother had prepared for this moment, however many books she had read, Jessica could hear the hurt in her voice. "Why not just wait a week or two? Take some time to absorb the situation," Jessica suggested.

"The apartment is ready. The Realtor has already listed the house. I'm going to get over to my fresh new place and out of here as soon as possible. It's too big for just me, anyway."

Jessica thought for a moment, glancing around the house, which looked like a rental home, devoid of mementos. Most of her mother's things were already over at the new place, with the exception of a few pictures and objects her father had wanted around.

It hurt Jessica to think how long her mother had been waiting for this day to come. "I need to move out of Cindy's place. What if I came and stayed with you for—"

"Absolutely not," her mother said, cutting Jessica off before she could even finish the sentence. "You know how your dad and I feel about you coming back to stay at home. You need to live your own life, be an independent woman who doesn't need her parents. You're lucky I'm letting you stay the night."

She knew her mother was just joking. Mostly. She wondered if her mom was using the familiar litany as a way to keep some sense of normalcy. Jessica ran her hand over the back of the old couch before walking over to her mother's side. "What can I do to help?"

A small smile flitted across her mother's face. "You can make us something to eat. Between fast food and the muck they served at the hospital, I haven't had anything decent in far too long."

Jessica nodded and turned toward the kitchen. Her mother called her name before she made it to the doorway. Jessica faced her mom.

"Jess, you better keep your word about what you said to your father. Don't let me or any of this stop you from getting out there and finding someone. Love's too important for that."

Jessica smiled at her mom. "I will."

She had no idea what she would do next, but she was at least sure of one thing: she wouldn't shy away from a chance at a lasting relationship, no matter what happened in the past or what could happen in the future.

12

AARON STORMED OUT of the barn, hardly noticing the sounds of the horses on either side. He didn't slow his pace until he'd walked to the small creek that went through his land. At the edge, he sat on a rock, the trees growing on the banks shading him from the winter sun, not allowing him even the small amount of warmth it afforded.

He could hear leaves crunch and the swish of brush on denim. Jeremiah had followed him, which he'd expected, but he didn't want to speak to anyone, not even his best friend. He tried to tell himself that a little peace and quiet would help, but he knew that wasn't true. It only made things worse.

He could see Jeremiah striding toward him out of the corner of his eye. "I don't want to talk about it," Aaron said.

Jeremiah crossed his arms. "Well, you're going to. You've been annoyed ever since Vegas, it seems, and I'm tired of it. Your whole 'I'm fine' thing, where you work yourself to the bone with earbuds blasting music while you ignore everyone? It isn't making things better, if you haven't figured it out. Tell me what's going on."

Aaron felt his frustration boiling. Why couldn't Jeremiah just leave him alone? Music and hard work were the only things that helped keep thoughts of Jessica out. He didn't want to think about her, but any moment his mind was free to wander, it always went back to her. He couldn't even read his book without picturing the way her eyes shone with excitement when he'd told her it was *Harry Potter*.

Jeremiah sat on the ground, even though it was probably cold and damp. "Seriously, Aaron. Just talk to me. I can help. What did that chick do to you in Vegas?"

She made me fall in love with her.

The thought came to him unbidden, unwanted.

Jeremiah spoke again, but Aaron was only half listening. "You need to deal with whatever issues that trip brought up if you ever want life to get back the way it was."

The way it was. That was what he had been trying to do for days. But he hated the way it was, now that he knew how it could be. Aaron had always thought of love as giving up independence, but what good was independence if the right person was out there and the only thing he could think of was how much it sucked not being with her because of a stupid misunderstanding?

Even if she didn't want to talk to him, he had to get in touch with her and try to set things right, see if there was any way to move past it. The past few days had made it abundantly clear that he was in it far deeper than he'd let himself believe. For years, he'd refused to become attached to a woman, and now here he was, completely addicted.

Not addicted. In love.

His mind knew it was ridiculous to feel that way about a woman he'd only known a few days, but his soul was stubborn. It was the first time he'd ever felt like that about anyone, and he wasn't going to just let that go.

He stood. "I need to talk to Jessica. I have to see if I can fix this."

Jeremiah asked, "How is talking to Jessica going to fix it?"

Jeremiah still seemed perplexed, so Aaron, almost gibbering as his mind rushed through the possible scenarios now that he'd made his decision, added, "Cody was right. I'm in love with her."

His heart felt lighter now that he'd admitted it aloud. Even if his quest was doomed to fail, he could at least tell her the truth.

Jeremiah's eyebrows disappeared into the hair falling over his forehead. "Seriously? Of all the things you could've said, that was not what I was expecting. And who the hell is Cody?"

Aaron shrugged. "A blackjack dealer. It doesn't matter. The point is, I need your help. Text that girl and get her to tell you where Jessica lives. I've got to talk to her, and I should do it in person."

He noticed that Jeremiah looked a little sheepish as he hauled himself off the ground. "So, the day after you left Vegas, before I got on my flight, I got a message from Marilyn. She said that Jessica was trying to find you and wanted your phone number. I told her no."

Aaron had to stop himself from strangling his best friend. Instead he pressed the heels of his palms into his eyes. "You're kidding, right?"

"I thought she was going crazy stalker on you, and that's why you bolted! You didn't exactly explain the situation. Hell, I still don't know what happened. That's why I've been sitting in mud for the past few minutes trying to get you to talk to me, dammit," he said, wiping at the butt of his jeans.

Aaron looked at his friend, really seeing him for the first time in days. The person who had been there for him practically his whole life, whom he'd ditched in Vegas without even explaining, was pissed. But he was still there, and he'd only been trying to help.

Aaron knew he'd been a terrible friend. "Look, Jeremiah, I'm sorry. I was falling for her and then she walked out on me. I tried to get her back, but she'd taken the next flight out of Vegas to get away from me. I was so frustrated I had to leave. I thought I could try to forget about her, but these past few days have been miserable. I need to see her again."

"Even though she left Vegas early just so she wouldn't have to see you again?"

"I need to explain some things. I have to at least try, right?"

Jeremiah looked at him for a second, then pulled out his phone. "Okay, grand gesture time. I get it. You really must be in love with her to do something this stupid. Do you want to go grab a bag together and I'll take you to the airport?"

Aaron slapped his friend on the back as Jeremiah tapped out a quick message and put the phone back in his pocket. They started walking toward Aaron's home.

Aaron wanted to run the moment he saw the large yellow house, no more than a quarter mile away, looming against the backdrop of the mountains, but this was no time to ditch his friend yet again. Jeremiah still seemed annoyed. Aaron said, "Thanks, Jeremiah. You're a good friend."

Jeremiah gave him a sidelong glance. "Way better than you've been."

Jeremiah's words were harsh, but he didn't sound too angry. It wouldn't take much to get him to come around. Aaron nodded. "*Way* better. I owe you so much beer."

That made Jeremiah smile, and Aaron felt better than he had in days. As they reached the house, Jeremiah tilted his head toward his truck. "Grab some stuff. I'll pull up to the front."

With that, Aaron took off, through the back door, up the stairs. He knew it was stupid, that this stuff only worked in the movies, and he was more likely than not going to be back in this quiet house, alone, within a few days. Still, he'd never felt more alive. He was rushing off to tell a woman he loved her, something he would have laughed at a couple of weeks ago.

He grabbed together a quick bag and the heaviest coat he owned. By the time he got back outside and locked the door, Jeremiah's truck was next to the porch, waiting for him. Aaron jumped into the cab and Jeremiah pulled away from the house, shaking his head, but grinning as he did so. He said, "Okay, I got an address. Apparently Marilyn doesn't know Jessica that well, but Jessica is roommates with Cindy, the bachelorette."

Aaron barely heard anything after the first sentence. He had her address. This was actually happening. He sat back in the seat, finally able to relax now that they were on their way, that he had a plan, as ridiculous as the plan was.

Jeremiah grew serious as they went through the gate that indicated the end of Aaron's driveway. "I don't want to rain on your parade or anything, but just don't get your expectations too high, okay? Remember when we read *Romeo and Juliet* in high school, and we talked about how idiotic it was that they'd known each other for three days? That's kind of you right now. I'm not saying it won't work out, I'm just saying—"

Aaron shrugged. He was very aware of how stupid he was being. "I know. I see why this is completely ludicrous. But I've been lying to myself, thinking I was happy, for long enough. Now that I've found what makes me actually happy, I have to go after it. And that's what I'm doing, even if it's a long shot."

His friend nodded. "Okay. Let's just stop by my place and I'll grab a couple of things and change into different pants. Shouldn't take two minutes."

Aaron looked at Jeremiah, who nodded decisively. "You think I'm going to let you do something this dumb on your own? Plus, I want to know what happens, and if I just send you off, the likelihood that I'll get even a text from you is slim to none. And I like New York. You'll go confess your love to the woman of your dreams, and I'll take a stroll around Central Park. Win-win."

Aaron laughed. "Awesome. I'm going to look up flights. We might not be in any rush if the next plane to New York doesn't leave for six hours or something."

He used his phone to find a flight that would give them enough time to get to the airport and through security, and booked two seats. Jeremiah got back in with his small duffel and they were once again on their way.

By the time they parked and began heading through to their terminal, Aaron had searched out Jessica's address location, booked two hotel rooms nearby, and ordered a car to pick them up at the airport. He'd even found a florist in case he wanted to get flowers, but he wasn't sure if that was sweet or going too far. He felt a strong affection for his phone as he put it on airplane mode for the flight. It had done its job well.

Now that Aaron was on the plane, though, enthusiasm started to give way to anxiety. What if she turned him down? What if she said she loved him, too, threw herself into his arms and then a month later changed her mind?

He told himself that if that happened, he would just have to go on. He couldn't let it stop him from trying.

Jeremiah was seated next to him, and was fidgeting as though he was nervous, which seemed strange. He wasn't the one going to declare his love to a woman he'd known for less than a week. Finally, once they were in the air and Jeremiah hadn't calmed down, Aaron turned to him. "Is everything okay? I thought you wanted to come with, but you're—"

"I want to come," Jeremiah cut in, "but I have something I need to say."

Aaron waited, dreading whatever his friend was going to say. He didn't want to hear about what a terrible idea this was; he already got that loud and clear.

After what felt like hours of awkward silence, Jeremiah started talking. "Look, in Vegas you were spending all your time with Jessica and I got annoyed. I told you I didn't like the way you were acting. Now, though, I can see that you were acting like an idiot in love, and that's kind of cool. So I guess what I'm trying to say is that I'm sorry."

That was definitely not what Aaron had expected. He almost said something nice back about how great Jeremiah was being about this whole thing, but he didn't have to. Jeremiah knew. Besides, it was becoming a bit too much of a bro-mance already.

He knocked his friend on the shoulder and leaned back in his seat.

At least he knew that if this thing went to pieces, Jeremiah would still be there to help him, just as he'd been when Aaron's parents divorced, when his mother died and a hundred other times.

The flight was over far sooner than Aaron had expected, and he steeled himself to get his heart smashed. He hoped it wouldn't happen, but he honestly wasn't sure. Yeah, she'd asked for his phone number, but there were plenty of reasons she could want it that didn't involve confessing undying love.

Jeremiah looked at him, raising one eyebrow. "You okay? Completely regretting this decision?"

"Nope to both. Let's go."

They found their way through the giant airport and to the waiting car. It was evening, but not too late. They drove straight over to her apartment, and the driver pulled up to the front door. "You still sure you want to do this?"

When Aaron nodded, he opened the door and stepped out, clearing the way. "Then go do it. I'll wait down here for ten minutes, then go to the hotel if I haven't heard from you. Good luck!"

Aaron was standing on the sidewalk, freezing, as the car door shut with a snap. He strode quickly toward the door, determined to do what he'd come there to do, whatever the consequences. He managed to catch the door before it shut as someone entered, allowing him to circumvent buzzing the apartment. He had no idea what he would have said. He still wasn't entirely sure what he would say. He went through her possible reactions and focused on the ones he liked the best, trying to decide how he would respond to each one.

He never found out what he would have said, though, because the moment the elevator doors opened at her floor, Jessica was pushing herself into it, a large cardboard box obscuring her vision. He was so shocked that he didn't say anything as she set down the box and stretched her back. She was in jeans that hugged every curve of her legs and a large baggy sweatshirt, her hair tied back in a messy ponytail, and she was so stunningly beautiful his heart clenched. Any doubts about his feelings were gone in an instant. He was in love.

JESSICA TURNED AWAY from the heavy box to make sure the ground-floor button was pushed, and jumped back in shock. Her leg hit the box, and a small cry escaped her as she lost her balance. Before she could catch hold of anything to stop her fall, Aaron's strong arms were around her, his handsome blue eyes staring into hers. There was another moment of silence before she finally gasped, "Aaron! What—"

She couldn't finish the sentence. Her thoughts hadn't yet caught up to the situation before her. His mouth turned up at the corners as he smiled. "Hi, Jessica. This situation seems familiar."

It took her several seconds before she realized what he meant. He was still holding her, the way he had when she bumped into him at the restaurant. Her mind started to slowly catch up. "You're in New York?"

It wasn't supposed to come out as a question, but somehow it did. He nodded. "I know this might seem a little crazy, but I needed to come tell you—"

Her brain was still struggling with the unexpected situation. "Wait, you're here at my apartment. How did you get here?"

"Jeremiah got the address from Marilyn. I had to talk to you."

"I asked for your phone number days ago, but Marilyn said that Jeremiah didn't want to give it to her. I thought you didn't want to talk to me. Now you're in New York to talk to me?"

She didn't mean to grill him, but it was all just so bewildering she couldn't help trying to wrap her mind around it all. The elevator dinged and the door closed, but neither of them moved from their impromptu hug to push a button.

"Jeremiah thought he was being helpful. I didn't know you wanted to talk to me. I thought you hated me and never wanted to see me again. I mean, you left Vegas just to get away from me. I waited outside your room the night you left, but you were already gone."

That brought reality crashing down. "I didn't leave because of you, Aaron. I got a phone call from my family. My dad was in the hospital. I had to come back."

His eyes filled with shock and empathy as he took in her words. "Is he okay?"

She smiled, but her eyes filled with tears. She was sad, but she'd had enough time to process the event that it wasn't overwhelming to answer. Besides, she wanted him to know. "He died. He'd been sick for a long time, but he finally passed away."

She found herself pressed against him as he hugged her close. She let her tears fall, his arms holding her, comforting her.

When the elevator began moving up, reacting to another tenant's call, she looked around, surprised to find herself in a small metal box. She had forgotten where she was. By his reaction, so had he. He looked at the doors for a second, then reached over quickly and hit the emergency button.

She laughed through her tears. "I don't think you're supposed to do that unless it's an emergency."

He tilted his head. "They can wait. Can I do anything to help?"

She snuggled closer to him. "You already have, and

I'm okay, really. We've known this was coming for a long time, and he was in a lot of pain, so… I just can't believe you're here. Why are you here?"

It had just occurred to her that it made absolutely no sense for him be in New York. If he found out she was trying to reach him, why didn't he just call?

"Well, this might be terrible timing now, but…" He took a deep breath, and she could feel his chest expanding against her body. "I came to tell you that I love you."

She stopped breathing. Before she could process and respond to it, he continued. "I know that's insane. I only met you a few days ago, we live thousands of miles apart and you're fully justified if you want to run away and never see me again. But I've never loved someone before and I had to tell you. I want to be with you, just you. If you have any feelings at all for me, I want to try to make this work somehow."

She was still silent. She had things to say but hadn't been able to find any way to say them, so she stood there, pressed against his chest. He exhaled. "I'm sorry, I know I shouldn't have said anything. You've got too much to deal with to worry about—"

His words cut off as she leaned up and kissed him, pressing her lips hard against his. He lifted her off her feet and kissed her back. She pulled her face back a fraction of an inch, just enough to look into his eyes and speak, her lips brushing against his. "I feel the same. Stupid, crazy, illogical as it all is." She pressed her lips back onto his.

The kiss quickly became deep and insistent, and she

had to pull away regretfully. "We're in the elevator. Probably not the best place for this. Any better ideas?"

"Back to your apartment, or to my hotel? The apartment's closer, but you have a roommate…" He looked at the box crowding the corner of the elevator. "Or are you moving out? Did I interrupt something?"

She looked at the box, remembering her mission. "Oh, right. Yeah, I am moving. Cindy's getting married in a few days, so I've been trying to get everything out before then. She's been really sweet about the whole thing and said I could stay as long as I want, but I'm ready."

He hit the emergency button again and then the one for the ground floor. The elevator began going upwards, continuing to its original destination. It opened to an empty floor, though. Apparently the person had given up and taken the stairs. They began their descent.

He picked up the box for her. "So, where are you moving?"

Jessica wasn't sure exactly what to say. "Well, I'm putting my stuff in storage and was planning on staying with my mom for a week, until after the funeral and Cindy's wedding. It's a weird week."

"And then?" he prompted, looking curious.

She blushed and looked down. "And then I was going to Texas. I promised my dad I'd try to find you."

The box shifted, nearly falling out of his hands, and she had to reach out to make sure it didn't crash to the floor. "You were going to *Texas*? As in, all of Texas?"

He was looking at her as if she were indomitable or crazy or something. She hoped it was the first option.

The elevator door opened, and they stepped into the lobby of her apartment building. She guided him outside into the cold.

There was a black car waiting outside, with Jeremiah sitting in it. The moment they walked through the building doors, he rolled down the window and waved. "Hi, Jessica!"

Aaron groaned quietly. "Jeremiah came with me." Louder, he said, "Things are good, Jeremiah. See you at the hotel later?"

The grin on Jeremiah's face widened. "Sounds good. You two have fun." He winked and turned to the driver, and the car pulled away.

Jessica felt as though she should be embarrassed, but the man seemed so good-natured that it was impossible. She and Aaron hurried down the street dodging the bags of trash and ice patches that littered the sidewalk, him carrying the large box.

"So, about Texas…" he prompted.

"Well, I had a plan," she explained. "I've looked up ranches that participated in the rodeo and started going through their websites looking for owners' names. I was pretty sure I could narrow it down to a few before leaving."

He looked impressed before he tilted his head, clearly curious again. "Wait, you promised your dad you'd find me? Why?"

She paused for a second before answering. This had gone too far for anything but complete honesty. "He said that I was different when I came back. I was sparkly. I don't know exactly what that means, but it was obviously because of you. He told me I should see you again. Before he died—" she cleared her throat, keeping her voice level "—I told him that I would try. So I was going to try."

They arrived at the storage facility a few buildings down, and she used her key to unlock the door. They walked the rest of the way to her unit in silence. She wasn't sure what else to say, so she waited, wishing he wasn't carrying anything so she could slip into his arms again.

Once he set down the box inside her nearly full storage unit, he turned toward her and enfolded her in a tight hug. Her heart was happy. She could almost hear her dad's approval. He spoke into her hair, his cheek leaning against her head. "So, do you still want to go to Texas, or do we need to find a place here?"

She moved back slightly so she could see his eyes. "Here? I thought you loved your ranch."

He lifted and dropped one shoulder. "I do, but I'm going to be here if that's where you are. There are plenty of people who can run the ranch just fine without me."

She smiled and snuggled closer to him. "Nah, it's too cold here. And I could use some open space. Let's try Texas. But we'll have to wait a week for all that."

"I'll be here. You'll be staying at your mom's, right? I'll find a room near her place, and you just let me know what you want me to do. I won't impose on your family time."

"Actually my mom's in the middle of moving and is very much of the mind-set that I should take care of myself. It'll make me stronger and whatnot." She leaned up to kiss him again, brushing her lips against his. "I think she'd like it if I was staying at a hotel nearby. Are you up for having a roommate?"

His lips told her everything she needed to know.

Epilogue

"YOU'LL HAVE FUN. Cindy would never make you do something that made you feel uncomfortable," Aaron said.

Jessica looked at him, skeptical, as she pulled her carry-on from the overhead bin. "Do you remember the dresses she made me wear at her bachelorette party?"

Aaron grinned. "Oh, I remember. Do you think she brought the black one with her? I wouldn't mind seeing that again. And underneath it—"

Jeremiah popped up from the row behind them and cut in before Aaron could finish the thought. "Whoa, dude, you're in public and I'm standing right here. In fact, I don't even care about the public thing. Just the me thing."

Jessica laughed. "Jeremiah, after the stories you've told us, and whatever I'm sure Aaron's shared with you, since when are you so squeamish?"

"Since you two became old almost-married people. Your sex life has probably degraded into some perverted deviant stuff just to keep it exciting. Or worse, completely boring. I don't want to hear it."

Aaron raised his eyebrows at his friend. "The first one, absolutely. Totally deviant."

"Really? Like what?" Jeremiah asked, leaning in.

Jessica sighed. "Guys, focus. Cindy's going to get me on a stripper pole or something, I just know it. Help me."

Aaron shrugged. "There's only like a fifty percent chance of that happening. Besides, remember how much fun you have when we go dancing? You love to dance. This time it'll just be with a stripper pole instead of me. That's awesome. Tell Cindy to send me pictures."

"And me!" chimed in Jeremiah, earning him an elbow in the ribs from Aaron. "What? As an amusing anecdote about my good friend Jessica. Not a sexual thing."

Once they were off the plane, Aaron wrapped his arm around Jessica's shoulders. Even after two years, it still made her melt to feel him so close. He leaned in to her, and her heart fluttered. How could it be possible that she was lucky enough to marry this man?

"We'll have a fun weekend. A little bachelorette party, a little rodeo. And you miss Cindy."

Jessica rested her head against his shoulder slightly. "I do miss her. I just know she has something crazy planned. I would never have guessed two years ago that I would be excited about going to a rodeo and nervous about spending time with Cindy."

"Of course you're excited about the rodeo. We're going to get first place this year."

Jessica answered, loud enough for Jeremiah to hear,

"We'll definitely get first place. Jeremiah doesn't stand a chance."

Jeremiah sped up so he was walking on the other side of her. "Just you wait, Jessica. You'll both be crying at the wedding, and not because of all the love or whatever. A week isn't going to be nearly enough time to get over how bad you're going to lose this weekend."

Jessica smiled at him. He was such a fun guy to have around. She could see why Aaron had been friends with him for so long.

Then she heard her name being screamed across the airport.

It could only be her best friend. She spotted Cindy running to her, and Jessica broke away from the boys to give her a tight hug. "I missed you!" Cindy said, squeezing her.

Jessica squeezed her back. It had been almost a year since she saw Cindy. Far too long.

AARON WATCHED THE GIRLS, happy that they were finally back together. Despite her worries, he knew that Jessica had missed her friend and was happy to be in the same city as her again.

Cindy turned to them, her arm still around Jessica. "Okay, boys. You do your thing, but Jessica's mine for this evening. We'll catch up with you at some point. Aaron, say goodbye to your bride-to-be. There's no promise she'll be coming back to you in one piece."

Jessica crossed the few feet between them and he enfolded her, bathing in her presence. She pressed her lips to his, and even that slight touch made him wish they were going to their room together, not separating for the evening.

As they broke apart, Jessica's eyes gazed into his, giving him the answer to his question. *Tonight*. He let her go with regret.

Then Cindy had Jessica by the arm and was bustling off. Jessica gave him one last look, mouthed a quick *I love you* and followed her friend. In just a few seconds, they were out of sight.

Jeremiah crossed his arms. "She seriously has no idea Cindy's pregnant?"

Aaron shrugged. "I didn't tell her, as per Cindy's orders. I think she wants Jessica to sweat until they get to dinner."

"I have no idea how you, her mom and her sister managed to keep that from her. When are they supposed to get here?"

"They arrived this morning, I think. If Cindy has everything as well planned as it seems, Jessica's going to be in for her perfect bachelorette party."

"A pleasant dinner with family and friends still doesn't sound like a bachelorette party to me," Jeremiah said.

Aaron nodded, but he knew Jessica would love it. And then she would come back to him tonight and they would have their own celebration in their room. It would be another amazing weekend in Vegas.

* * * * *

COMING NEXT MONTH FROM

HARLEQUIN *Blaze*

Available January 19, 2016

#879 A SEAL'S TOUCH
Uniformly Hot!
by Tawny Weber

Cat Peres wants to help her childhood crush Taylor Powell, now a
sexy SEAL and struggling with some very grown-up problems. But
he keeps pushing her away...even as he pulls her into his arms.

#880 ONE SIZZLING NIGHT
Three Wicked Nights
by Jo Leigh

Logan McCabe, security expert, is on assignment. Kensey Roberts
has a mission of her own, which clashes with Logan's. They both
need to keep their objectives under wraps...too bad they can't say
the same about themselves!

#881 COWBOY CRUSH
by Liz Talley

Maggie Stanton hires the sexiest cowboy she's ever seen to
help her get her ranch ready to sell. But the heat between them
has Maggie wanting more from her temporary employee. And
Cal Lincoln is willing to oblige...

#882 NAKED PURSUIT
The Wrong Bed
by Jill Monroe

When Stella wakes up with no memory of the past night and
handcuffed to a gorgeous firefighter, she has to find out what
happened. So she and Owen decide to re-create the night—
each crazy, sexy moment...

HBCNM0116

Taylor Powell pulled his Harley into the driveway and cut
the engine.

Home.

He headed for the front door, located his key and
stepped inside.

"Yo," he called out as the door swung shut behind him.
"Ma?"

He heard a thump then a muffled bang.

"Ma?" His long legs ate up the stairs as he did a quick
mental review of his last CPR certification.

As he barreled past his childhood bedroom, he heard
another thump coming from the hall bathroom. This time
accompanied by cussing.

Very female, very unmotherly, cussing.

In a blink his tension dissipated.

He knew that cussing.

Grinning he sauntered down the hall. Stopping in the
bathroom door, he smiled in appreciation of the sweetly
curved rear end encased in worn denim.

The legs were about a mile long. The kind of legs that went beyond wrapping around a guy's waist.

He almost groaned when his eyes reached a pair of black leather boots similar to the ones he wore on duty. Was there anything sexier than legs like that in black boots?

"Hellooo," he murmured.

"What?" The hips moved, the back arched and the owner of those sexy legs lifted her head so fast he heard it hit something under the sink. Rubbing her head, the woman glared at him with enough heat to start a fire.

"Taylor?"

"Cat?" he said at the same time. He started to help her to her feet, but at the last second paused. Touching her so soon after that image of her legs wrapped around him didn't seem like a smart idea.

When the hell had Kitty Cat gotten hot?

Her golden hair was tied back, highlighting a face too strong to be called pretty. Eyes the color of the ocean at sunset stared back under sharply arched brows. The rounded cheeks and slight upper bite were familiar.

The way her faded green tee cupped her breasts was new, as was the sweetly gentle slide from breast to waist to hip where the tee met denim.

Oh, yeah. Kitty Cat was definitely hot.

"Hey there, Mr. Wizard," Cat greeted. "Still out saving the world?"

"As always. How about the Kitty Cat?"

"Same as ever," Cat said with a shrug that did interesting things to that T-shirt of hers.

Things he had no business noticing…

Don't miss A SEAL'S TOUCH by Tawny Weber, available February 2016!

HARLEQUIN®

A *Romance* FOR EVERY MOOD™

JUST CAN'T GET ENOUGH?

Join our social communities
and talk to us online.

You will have access to the latest
news on upcoming titles and special
promotions, but most importantly,
you can talk to other fans about your
favorite Harlequin reads.

Harlequin.com/Community

 Facebook.com/HarlequinBooks

Twitter.com/HarlequinBooks

Pinterest.com/HarlequinBooks

THE WORLD IS BETTER WITH

Romance

7203

Harlequin has everything from contemporary, passionate and heartwarming to suspenseful and inspirational stories.

Whatever your mood, we have a romance just for you!